MW01115435

Black Love Matters

A Crazy, Sexy Urban Love Story

By Quardeay

Copyright © 2018 Quardeay

Published by Tiece Mickens Presents, LLC

All rights reserved. No part of this book may be reproduced in any form without written consent of the publisher, except brief quotes used in reviews.

This is a work of fiction. Any references or similarities to actual events, real people, living or dead, or to real locals are intended to give the novel a sense of reality. Any similarity in other names, characters, places, and incidents are entirely coincidental.

About the Author

I was born in the small city of Milwaukee, Wisconsin. I am a Journalism Major getting ready to transfer to the University of Milwaukee Wisconsin to continue my education. At 24 years old, I have published 11 titles so far with plans to expand into screenwriting very soon. The love I have for Urban Fiction and the company I work for TMP are astronomical.

When I first began my writing career, I didn't think that I would last in this industry. There were times that I wanted to quit on my dreams and there were times that I didn't want to go further because of some of the negativity that I would see being exhibited amongst it. However, I knew once I began to connect with several other literary phenoms that my place was right here.

I love being able to entertain people all around the world with my words and make women smile with my projects. I've learned to adapt to every element and turn my pain into pleasure for all my readers. My journey is only beginning and as I get older, I see only brighter days on the horizon. I may not be your favorite author, but I want to be the one you will never forget.

Quote

Like the great J. Cole once said, "I'm God Blessed, and I'm a Success."

Acknowledgements

This is dedicated to:

The TMP family that has made me one of their own for a year now. You have all been my heartbeat, and I owe you all the world.

My publisher, *Tiece Mickens*, who has turned my dream into a reality.

Taniqua Julien, my loving mother.

Kegan Julien, my supportive uncle.

Brenda Julien, my loving grandmother. To the friends who know me the best and have had my best interest at heart.

To everyone who has been there for me through the years:

Timone Mccloud

Stephen Henry

Micheal Lucas

Stacey West

Buck Brooks

Delorian "Delo" Diggs

Dejah Campbell

Mario Calvin

Liyah Sumner

Lydia Maury

Shanice Swint

Shantel Sanders

Mike Wilder

Walter Jack Lanier

Tyeshia Quinn

Rodney And Ronnie Allen

Donovan Lassiter

Sarah Smith

Ashley and Destiny Blair

Myles Blackstar

Okeema Ikanih and Carlos Gamble

Reginald Adams and Morgan Walker

Tim Brown Jr.

To fellow authors that have been an inspiration to me over the years with their work and help:

Myah

China White

Vee—My best friend in the writing world.

Shaniya Dennis

Christina Deer

Zane

Eric Jerome Dickey

Bre Marshall

Melissa St. Julien.

Author Na'Kia

Maria Harrison-My Favorite Editor in the world!

Paree Tranae

Shakela James

Jeffery Roshell

AJ Dix

Taylor Kirk

Words from the Author:

I would like to thank you for taking the time to read my latest project. I consider this one of my best projects yet, and I believe that all who reads this will enjoy the words on every page. I would also like to thank you for your patience in allowing me to stay dedicated to my craft. Every book that I write is for the enjoyment of all of you. I would also like to dedicate this to those I've lost: Jay Anderson, Mary Jones, Tsavia Baker, Jamille Julien, and Ernest Handford.

To the memories of Trayvon Martin, Kenneka Jenkins, Sandra Bland and millions of others that were coldly taken away from us before they could really bless us with their presence.

I would also like to dedicate this novel to every strong, BEAUTIFUL educated black woman out in the world. I hate the way that the world demeans you, disregards your worth, and underrates your importance. If nobody else says this to you, I will, **I am so proud of you all.** *You are man's greatest addiction. You all mean so much to me as a man because without your integrity, honor, and grace, where would we as men be? Thank you for simply being who you are and trust me, all of you hard* *work doesn't go unnoticed. I love you my Queens. This one is for you.*

Peace and Love, Quardeay

Black Love Matters

For two people, Black Love is defined by their never-ending love making that's as hot as a ray from the Sun. For two others, it's their mental ecstasy that combines them as one.

Meet Philly Washington, a sexy, successful business woman who seems to be in a constant battle with herself. Despite having many men after her and the little slice of heaven between her legs, no one seems to be Mr. Right. And Philly knows exactly what Mr. Right will look like, or so she thinks. Her guidelines and requirements for a man are thrown out when the suave and mysterious Avant Moore enters her life, matching her in every way possible including her insane sex drive. One night brings the two together and takes them on a wild ride they never saw coming.

As Philly searches out the perfect man, her artistically gifted best friend Parker Massey is along for the ride. Nothing like Philly, Parker is a virgin who is never indulged in physical pleasure and has no interest in giving it up to the dogs whom seem to sense her virginity the way that a shark senses blood. But that changes when she comes across the equally innocent; Khali Carter who's only love comes from a canvas and his paints. Their meeting starts a soul snatching love affair that no one would've seen coming and unravels some secrets better kept in the dark.

  With lust and secrets under every sheet, will these women ultimately find love? Or will it all become too much to take on? No matter what, in the end all four of these individuals will find out the true meaning of why Black Love Matters.

Black Love is everything to me

It's the R&B song that I keep on repeat

It's the first and last piece of chocolate inside a heart shaped box

It's the flow of water coming from the sea

Black Love is the greatest sight that you'll ever see.

--Khali Carter

Part 1

The Ladies Of LA

Chapter One

Philly

Let's make one thing perfectly clear right now, I LOVE SEX! But that does not make me a HOE, THOT, SLUT, or TRICK. I fuckin' hate words like that. Those are the worst labels that can be slapped on a woman.

Is there truly something wrong with loving sex? Sex has never hurt me nor will it ever. Now, I've been told by my cousin and my best friend that I needed to check myself into some type of facility because they thought that I was a bonafide sex addict. Yeah right.

I've told them several times that I have no problem with getting busy every night of the week because it's a stress relief and it's just me having a little harmless fun. I give men what they really what from me with no strings attached and then I carry on with everyday life. Does that make me a hoe? Hell no! If men can fuck as many women as they want than surely, I can do the same. I would love to do it without being a victim of some double standard labeling by a sensitive, dry dick male.

Ugh. It's the worst but still I rise as Maya Angelou once said.

So, who am I you ask? Well, that's a question that many ask and even when answered they still don't have them all figured out.

My name is Philandria Washington but at a young age my father nicknamed me "Philly" because of the love he had for the state itself. I learned so much from my time in Philadelphia, the streets practically helped me understand who I am. I'm a self-confident, strong willed woman with a heart, body, and brain that were strong enough to knock over a building.

I'm one of the executive writers for Essence Magazine so you've probably seen my fashion and sex advice column *The Queen's Throne*. It's like an urbanized version of something you would see out of Cosmo. I've written articles about everything from, if size matters, to what you shouldn't say in the bedroom when in mid-romp. So, as you can probably guess, sex is a very big part in my life. You could say that it's my bread and butter. I do what I can to educate strong black women every single time I write an article.

Everyone has an opinion about me and that's fine. If you hear it from my judgmental mother, she'd say that I was a thirty-year old woman with no morals and no self-value which is bullshit. My best friend Parker would say that I'm a nympho who hid behind the sheets that I laid in because I was too afraid to confront the pain in my past. *Bullshit yet again.* If you hear from my past flings, they'll say that I'm a know it all, self-absorbed freak. *Bullshit.*

In my mind, I consider myself to be a free spirited pansexual Libra woman with a life that many others dreamed that they had. Now that doesn't mean that I'm letting every man with a penis in L.A hit my cherry pie, I do have standards. In fact, I have very strict standards, and not too many men can fit that mold. It wasn't my fault that when I gave men the business they fell in love with me.

I mean, who wouldn't want me? I'm five feet two, my cocoa butter complexion is as clear as water with not a pimple in sight, and my ass is tight and soft enough for a nigga to sleep on. I was a thirty-year old who could pass for twenty-one any day. I could have any man, and I could have their daddy too. Hell, I could have their granddaddies wanting to pay my mortgage until he takes the trip to the upper room.

Okay, now back to these strict standards.

For one, I rarely give the opportunity to any man who refers to a woman as their "bitch" or their "hoe." Like who do you think you are? What gives you the right to label a woman with such animalistic taglines? Now I say rarely because there was one man that slid past the initial testing after his application passed. His name was James Wells, and he was a fine piece of Hershey's chocolate. I mean this man had it all. He was a stock broker out of Fresno with a Master's in Business.

Yeah, he was a Master of Business alright because this man had a stroke that could make your body vibrate for weeks. When he would stick it inside of me, James would make me scream to other continents and make me squirt puddles. James used to do things that would make me wonder if he had been a porn star in his past life. One night I remember him licking honey from each of my nipples and then slurping some from around my belly button as my body shivered in ecstasy. James would break me off so good that I would often find myself checking my heartbeat to see if I were still alive. His touch alone could make you cream your panties.

Damn he was so majestic with his spine-tingling touch and his kisses that could melt you like a frozen strawberry shortcake over a bonfire.

The way that James would bury his face in between my thighs and suck each of my pussy lips before gliding his tongue from outer space inside of me would bring tears to my eyes.

Here's where the ULTIMATE problem began with me and Mr. James. James began to get way too comfortable with me and it showed when this bastard thought it was a good idea to call me out of my name when we were having a VERY volatile argument. I must tell you that when I heard the word "bitch" leave his chapped ass lips, I instantly got the urge to make some hot grits to throw all over his lap.

Hmm, I don't think his hair has ever grown back on that side of his pubes either. Welp, too bad. I really did like James, but I didn't, nor will I ever tolerate being referred to by any word that isn't *Queen, Goddess, or Philly.* James wasn't the only man to miss out on this good loving either.

When I first met Skills, and yes, his name was really Skills, he was only twenty-four. At that age I know that he was still trying to find himself. What I liked in Skills aside from his fro that made him resemble a young Maxwell was his wit. That man could make me laugh like I was at a comedy show. He was so corny that it was attractive. I guess it would be cliché to say that those weren't his only "*Skills*" that he had in his arsenal.

I had never been orally pleased while hanging upside down from someone's shoulders until I met Skills. That man was an oral genius with the way that his tongue worked on my clitoris that I could've married his tongue alone if it would've proposed. Just thinking about how his mouth game could cause this sensual affliction onto me could make goosebumps dance all over my body. Skills was so passionate in the bedroom, he was a fierce young lion that would take his time eating his prey. My pretty, polished toes would often tangle together as he kissed every inch of my exposed skin under the dimmed lights.

I would put this on his young ass so much that I was starting to feel addicted to his juicy lips, pulling on his unkempt fro as I rode his eight-inch dick until the early morning, and making him let out a manly moan that brought out an evil smile to my devious face. I used to fuck the absolute existence out of that child.

The problem with Skills was that he still lived with his mother and while I could understand how a younger male could remain dependent on his childhood home due to finances or school, so I let him slide for the most part. I mean, besides, it was something about sneaking into his basement and having this dirty, little sexual affair that was kind of a turn on to me.

Yeah, that was until mommy dearest was standing over us as I was riding his dick, just about to climax by the way. There was nothing weirder than a woman who was wondering why a thirty-year-old woman was banging their junior in college son whilst calling him daddy very loudly and very passionately mind you. Let me tell you, I was way too old to be running from a basement with one shoe on and a momma chasing me with a broom.

As you could probably imagine, that little romance ended faster than you could say MILF. Which is why I added a new rule to my list; NO MORE MOMMA'S BOYS. EVER! Well, it was fun with little boy blue while it lasted, I suppose.

So where did that leave me now you ask?

Well after months of trying to connect with new suitors, the only dick that was going inside of me currently was a vibrating one because that was the only one I had nearby. I felt like a new age Eve looking for her Adam to chew on her apple again. Sometimes I considered, and I do mean truly considered going on social media to act a fool in one those groups.

You know those Beard Gang Matters type groups where all the sistahs go to play in their pussies to facially blessed men when their boyfriends were asleep? Yeah, I was getting so desperate for some good loving that I was practically stalking groups like that to look for my next victim. I knew I had a problem when I was sliding in inboxes trying to see what was up with some of these little daddies.

I needed some pleasure immediately, something new, hot, fresh, and something ripe. I wanted to feel the warmth from another body as the sweat dripped from our bodies and we created something magical between the sheets. Sadly, the only thing hot that I was getting tonight aside from my vibrator was my hot cup of Ramen with a dash of Cajun seasoning inside of it. It was a Friday night and I was sitting perched in between my couch next to my pit bull puppy Sweetheart watching a Love & Hip Hop rerun.

My head was truly banging trying to figure this show out. I mean, I got it for the most part, a bunch of catty singers trying to relieve the glory days of a few one hit wonders by acting an ass on TV. You have to get paid somehow, I guess, I just feel like it demeans talented black individuals who could be doing a lot more to get their name out there again. Maybe I was thinking too much into it.

I finished my soup and got up to go to the kitchen for more food because when I was horny, I became hungrier than usual. I pulled out a container of juicy, red strawberries and the remainder of my Cool Whip before heading to my laptop. I figured if I wasn't getting any action, then I could at least get some work done. Another one of my favorite hobbies consisted of writing erotic short stories on my personal website.

It was another way for me to get mine off from a mental standpoint when I wasn't getting it from the physical. I loved being able to intensify the emotions of my audience by making sweet, methodical love to their souls with my word play. I put on Mya's *Love Is Like* before typing up a quick paragraph.

I took you upstairs and led you to the bedroom where your bath awaited inside the bathroom. I helped you undress and then lit your cigar as you got into the hot water. I brushed your wavy hair as you smoked your cigar, and then I put on Ab-Soul, your favorite artist.

I let you relax as I got things ready inside of the bedroom. I lit more candles and then went down to the downstairs bathroom to wash off myself. I came back to the bedroom while pulling out body oil and your du-rag. I waited for you to finish before bringing your fione ass to the bedroom and telling you to sprawl across the sheets.

You did as I asked, and I then rubbed you down with the body oil as I sang softly into your ear. You were starting to fall asleep. I could feel your body starting to fall under hypnosis. I woke you back up by kissing the sides of your neck and then kissing between your shoulder blades. I assisted you with turning over onto your back, as I began to kiss your pecs.

"I admire you so much. I would be purposeless without you." I said as my kissing became lower and lower.

You gave me a manly moan, and then I watched your dick begin to rise like a mountain. I stroked your dick with both of my hands; it was so big, so thick.

Your eyes were closed tightly, your breathing became heavy, and you were so ready to be pleasured that you were already positioning so that my face was near your fat dick.

I teased you by kissing it a bit. I made you wait for it. You were so ready for me; you could just feel it coming. Well, ask and you shall receive. I then began to kiss your tip; your body started to shiver. I then licked round your shaft; your body was now convulsing. Your trance was complete after I placed it into my mouth and swallowed as much of it as I could.

I told you this was your night and that's what I meant. I wanted you to feel good. I wanted you to feel secure. Whatever you desired, I would supply you. My mouth went to work on your meat, stroking up and down as you craved more. You were so shaken. Your soul was taken and your body belonged to me. I continued to suck you down until you felt me stop.

I wasn't done with you yet. I was ready to make you cum inside of me. I straddled you, kissing you until you felt me slip you inside of my hot, juicy, wet walls as you groaned out in passion. I loved feeling you inside of me. It felt so good, so thick, so big and you knew that a shorty like me could take all of it in stride.

I rode you until my pussy could take no more, tightening my walls around it, making you work to make me cum as you came countless times that night. You went to sleep that night a pleased man and I went to sleep a proud woman knowing that my man could trust in me to make your night better than your day could've ever been.

--- Philly.

As soon as I finished, I closed my laptop and took a big bite from one of my strawberries while admiring my work. I got this very orgasmic thrill from writing out my biggest fantasies and driving my readers wild. It was the same feeling that I got from the bedroom itself when I turned off those lights and gave the person lucky enough to be there with me what they were asking for.

That was the problem. That was the fucking problem.

The more I sat in the house on this night feeding readers my words, the more that I would torture myself with a lack of sensuality. I needed SEX. Now sure I had people that I could call up. I had a whole phonebook full of people in phone. But I knew that even with a one-night stand, I'd probably regret banging any of them again. It would be like if you really wanted a cup of milk knowing that you're lactose intolerant, but you drink it anyway because your throat is drier than the Sahara Desert. You know it's a dumb move but you're desperate so you do it anyway only to feel sick the next morning as a result.

So, what's a woman to do? My phone was at the point of dehydration and my pussy was too, I decided that the only way that I'd be able to really get the passion that I was begging for was if I hit the clubs in search of it.

I picked up my phone and decided to ring up my boo Parker and my whacky ass cousin Janae to see if they wanted to step out with me. I hadn't been to *Club Joi* in a while, and that was where I usually met some fine bachelors looking for a good time for the night. Janae's crazy ass would be down for sure because one thing that she would never turn down was getting the chance to get drunk and meet somebody she could take home.

Parker would be the true test because she wasn't big on the club scene. She was an introvert who got her vibes from being inside of someone's poetry café or an art gallery. I could respect her drive, but that girl needed to get laid badly. Maybe then she could understand why I loved sex as much as I did. Parker was so judgmental at times that I didn't even like going to her about my sexual escapades because she would turn up her nose at me.

Chapter Two

Parker

The Los Angeles sky was so beautiful at night. I was practically in a trance gazing deep into it as the elegant stars slowly danced around my pupils. I spent most nights like this, bathing in nature's ebony glaze with the steam from a hot cup of Chai Tea rising up into my nostrils. Often nights I stayed up looking into the sky daydreaming of finding the right man for me.

Don't get me wrong, California was full of attractive men with beautiful black and white skin that you just wanted to rub your face on. However, under the surface was the fur from the dogs that they truly were within.

It seemed more like a distant fantasy though because I was something of a hopeless romantic. Sure, I had met my fair share of men, but it only went so far once they got to know me. I had to face the facts that most men weren't up for dating a 28-year-old virgin, church girl who wanted to be the next great artist in Cali. The ones who actually wanted to stick around were only sticking around because they thought they stood a chance to actually "break" my virginity like some type of sick conquest. If only people could've heard some of the lines that men would throw at me to get me into my bed, they were sick.

I had heard everything from; *"Yo baby, how about we stop talking and start bumping uglies."*

To this hidden gem; *"Baby. You're so fine. You don't have to do anything. Just let me smell the coochie and I'll be satisfied."*

I can't forget this one; *"Baby I know you're an artist so how about I make my tongue the paintbrush and your body the canvas."*

To my personal favorite; *"Okay, since I took you to dinner, how about you repay me with some mouth action."*

Man. Men could be such dogs. Hell, they could be worse than the average dog actually because at least most dogs listened to you and respected you. LA had a few good ones though, they just weren't checking for me. Either all of the good ones were already in a relationship or they were seeking after some skinny hot chick with a mini skirt and high heels to which I could never be.

I'll admit that I wasn't the skinniest chick on the block. I was a 5'5, 132-pound caramel skinned woman and I felt like I had curves for days. It's not easy being more on the plus size side sometimes because I'm so self-conscious. I always felt like I'm not enough for men to really grow an attraction to. Philly would always tell me that I looked good but that was probably just her trying to keep my spirits up. Deep down, I used to feel really fat and ugly. Mainly because the last relationship that I actually had was with a guy named Scorpio and initially everything was cool between us until things went south of the border.

Once Scorpio knew that I wanted to wait to have sex until I knew that he was what I truly wanted, he began to rebel and treat me horribly. Scorpio would down me for gaining weight and make me feel hideous, so I began to feel like such. I hated myself, but once I got rid of him I reconnected with God and learned to love myself again under his mercy.

Now I walked with a higher self-esteem and any man that enters my life had to be able to accept me for who I am because I wasn't willing to change myself for any man no matter how cool, sexy, and fit he was. Maybe that's why I was single. I was so protective of myself that I was fighting with the idea of actually letting someone in again just to be let down.

It hurt though. I really wanted to fall in love and I really wanted to know what it was like to have a man who didn't want to lose me. I guess it was all a fantasy for now. A fantasy that I was addicted to having come to fruition. For now, I was solely focused on my art work. I had been illustrating paintings since I was fifteen and my biggest inspiration came from my dad who himself was a famous poet and artist. I would spend hours in my room creating masterpieces and trying to sell them to art galleries.

No luck so far, but I wasn't giving up so easily. I was going to keep my head in the sky until one of these paintings paid off and my dreams truly came true. Until then, my house would look like Picasso threw up in it. I had so many stunning paintings and hand-crafted creations in my house I could've advertised it as a museum. One of my favorites was the one that I painted with Obama waving to the people and Malcolm X looking down from Heaven smiling while playing chess with Martin Luther King Jr.

I tried to sell that beauteous piece to this one saddity art gallery in South L.A, the *PANACHE GALLERY*, but was told that it would be too controversial. I felt like that was their way of trying to tell me that my black work wouldn't sell and they wanted no parts of it. It was moments like that one that kept me invested in my work because I wanted nothing more than to see my hard work observed for the world to see.

I was going to prove that I was a strong, talented black woman who could do anything that she set her mind too. Contrary to what the naysayers thought.

As I inhaled the cool air and allowed my body to be at one, I could hear my phone vibrating against the cold pavement from my porch. I looked down to see that it was Ms. Philly calling with her wild self. That child was something else. I didn't understand how she could give herself to all of those men and not have a stitch of feelings for any of them.

I picked up my phone and answered the way that I always did with her.

"What's up little mama?" I said enthusiastically.

Philly then said back over the line, "Nothing girl. Bored isn't even half of the word to describe me right now. I feel like I'm dying over here. My coochie is dry and unpenetrated. Girl I need some action."

I laughed before saying, "You need some saving that's what you need."

She sighed, "Whatever girl don't start. You know I've never gone this long without some action. I mean damn girl, it's Friday and I feel like I'm missing out on life. Let's do something."

"Like what girl?"

"Like going out. It's Friday night and *Club Joi* is calling my name."

Now I loved me some Philly, God knows I do but this woman needed to grow up a bit. We weren't as young as we used to be, the club wasn't my style, and she knew that. I only went with her because it was her scene and I loved seeing her happy. I took a deep breath and thought about an excuse that I could come up with so that I didn't have to go. I quickly scratched that because Philly could always sniff out a lie. So I just sucked it up before giving her the answer that she sought.

"Okay girl, let's see what's up tonight."

"You sure girl?"

"Yes. I'm sure." I said reluctantly said as I sipped my tea. "I'll go and get dressed."

"YASS. Okay, I'll be around to get you in an hour. Get that sexy body ready baby. The men are calling our name tonight. See you in a bit."

I shrugged and stood up from my seated position to begin getting ready for another crazy night with Philly. Every time I went out with her, I always ended up either watching her make out with some random bar patron or I was holding her hair as she puked all over my shoes. One time, I actually held her shoes for her as she topped some guy off in the bathroom stall after mingling with him all night.

Needless to say, that I had some crazy experiences going out with Philly, hopefully tonight would be a little bit different. I really wanted Philly to get her life together because at her age she shouldn't really be out acting as if she were still a preteen but because I vowed to always be her rock and the Bible preaches patience I remained by her side no matter how many times I want to shake her.

I allowed *Floetry* to put my mind at ease as I pulled out a velvet dress that had a slit between the thigh and threw it on the bed. My cat Humphrey walked into the room and purred near my legs. It seemed like he was the only real man that I had in my life at any juncture which was kind of sad actually because I never pictured myself being one of those cat ladies that I see on TV.

After my shower, I got dressed and put on some make up as I looked into the the mirror to admire my body. I traced my finger over the few stretch marks covering the bottom of my butt and thought to myself while posing in the mirror, *"Damn, I make stretch marks look so good. Keep your head up girl."*

After getting dressed and spraying myself with a few squirts of Versace perfume, I heard the sound of Philly's horn coming from outside. I quickly zipped up my thigh high leather boots and scurried outside where Philly was sticking half her body out of the window while she promiscuously danced to Beyoncé's 1+1. I shook my head in shame as she stuck her body back inside of her red Mercedes Benz, obviously she was already buzzed from her pre-turn up.

Philly looked very gorgeous though, she was sporting a tight black dress as ebony as the sky and her usually straightened hair was curled up at the ends. Not to mention, she was rocking black lipstick to match.

"WHAT'S UP GIRL?" she screamed before hugging me and handing me her bottle of pineapple Malibu.

"Go ahead and take a hit of that baby. You know we can't go without being influenced already."

"Girl you are bugging." I said before taking a quick sip. I wasn't much of a drinker. I usually only had a glass of wine or two when at home. However, whenever I was around Philly, I always found myself throwing back a shot or two or ten. Sometimes she could be such a bad influence on me, it was crazy.

I looked behind me before asking, "Where's Janae?"

Philly quickly answered back, "Oh she didn't answer the phone. I don't know if she's sleep or getting piped down already but I wasn't waiting around for her. It's just me and you tonight."

"Oh, well you just make sure that I'm not carrying you back to the car tonight girl. I'm not wearing the right shoes for it."

"What?" Philly said partially offended. "That's such an unfair statement. I'm the perfect angel when I'm out with you."

I laughed and immediately shut that down. "Baby girl please, between you and Janae I don't know which one is worse. You've done everything from flash the club while standing on the bar to actually punching one of the bartenders for forgetting the lime for your margarita. Please Philly, stay cool tonight."

Philly rolled her eyes and shrugged. "Okay girl. I will."

"You promise?"

"I promise."

I knew she was lying. I was already prepared to jump to her aid when the inevitable happened. I took a deep breath and sat back to enjoy the chill music as the few sips of liquor that I had taken began to run through me. I loved Philly's taste in music, it fit her so well, spunky but fresh. One minute she'd be jamming to some Beyoncé and then the next minute she'd be playing some TLC straight like that. I couldn't help but nod my head when I heard Salt and Pepa start blasting from her radio.

Boom baby baby. Boom baby baby.

If anyone ever got into the car with her, they'd be in the zone within seconds. If you were in a mood, she'd be sure to get you out of it by playing something that could speak to your current state of mind. I was starting to feel myself getting into the moment and I was starting to think that this would be a great night after all.

We found a sweet little parking spot by the entrance of the *Club Joi* and squeezed in between two cars before checking our make-up.

"You ready for this girl?" Philly asked to me exuberantly.

"Yeah, I think."

"You have your I.D right?"

"Naw." I answered back sarcastically. "I let Humphrey borrow it. What you think girl?"

Philly smiled and placed her hands in front of her face. "Okay. Okay. I'm sorry killer, don't beat me up. Come on, let's get in line before it gets packed up there."

Part 2

The Big

Move

One Day Before

Chapter Three

Avant

The last thing that I said before I boarded my flight was, "Goodbye Atlanta. See you on the flip side."

It seemed kind of surreal to me because I had been in Georgia since I was a child and I damn near bled waffle batter from Roscoe's. I took one last look at the city that had given me everything and blew a kiss to it before I stepped onto the humid first-class floor of the plane taking me to Los Angeles. My bags were so heavy that it felt like I was carrying two bodies inside of them or something. That was a bit morbid I know but that's how it felt.

Once I put my bags into the storage space above my head, I plopped down near the free window seat and looked out of the window as the stars above glowed like fireflies. I closed my eyes to pray for a safe flight. I was always so hesitant to fly I had a death fear of heights. But this was one trip that I was willing to take countless times especially with what was awaiting me in the City of Angels.

Let me explain, I've been writing manuscripts since I was fifteen. I'm an English major that graduated with my master's from Morehouse University and my dream was always to write for a newspaper or magazine. Now initially, I sent feelers to random magazines just trying to test my luck only to find out that I had no luck. It all changed when I sent my resume and application to *Essence* to become one of their newest writers. I had this idea of bringing my fiction work to the magazine, maybe as a way to really reinvent the brand itself.

I thought that it would be a waste of time though. I mean if little rinky-dink magazines wouldn't accept me then I was sure that a big baller brand like *Essence* wouldn't either. Long story short, it ended up being the best thing that happened to me because I got a call back within a week's time. Apparently, the last writer won the lottery and said, "Screw the job I'm going to Maui. Deuces."

It's funny how fate works.

Now here I was sitting on this plane, hungry and anxious but ready to see what the world was about to bring to me. As I prepared for takeoff, I pulled out my laptop to check out my emails before pulling up Microsoft Word to start up a poem to keep me busy. While writing erotica was my true cup of coffee, I did enjoy breaking out some erotic poetry every now and then to soothe my mental. It wasn't my calling but more of a seductive mating call so to speak.

I love sex. I know a lot of people say that but with me, sex was a sweet piece of chocolate on a fall night by the fireplace. Everything about sex attracts my aura, the energy that comes with it, the passion, the friction, the danger, the risk. When choosing my sex partners, I always find something about them that can make me want to come back for a second round whether it's their smile, it's their body, their feet, their hair, no matter the pro, I make my need to please them. I would often have one-night stands with chicks that I met at clubs and it was something I got used to.

I was what you would call a *Professional Freak.* There was nothing that I wouldn't do to please the woman that was lucky enough to enter my bedroom for a round or two. Once they entered, they'd never be the same. I will suck their toes, licking between each corner until they shiver. I will tongue kiss their clitoris with an ice cube in my mouth until their bodies ascend to Heaven for a two-night trip, and I would even take a peek into the backdoor to lick around the rim.

Fellas, don't judge me. Hear me out for a second, I will be honest. I was against the idea of putting my mouth towards the backdoor until I saw how this one chick reacted when I did it. I will do anything to bring a lady to the orgasm that she truly desires.

It's pretty easy to get women to attract to me. I'm five feet ten with the body of a linebacker and the tongue game of a mythical God. If my thick beard, wavy hair, and muscular frame didn't bring them to me, I only had to say one simple phrase to say to them, "I'm a writer." Once I said that, they would immediately urge me to read them something or recite some type of poetry which only ended up getting me into their pants once I aroused them with my sensual word play that bounced off of them like a rubber ball.

I could make women fall in love with me based off of my verbal flirtation alone, it wasn't hard to please them elsewhere either.

I thought back to the last fling that I had before leaving. It was with a chick named Kassidy, Kassidy Williams. Kassidy was this beautiful, tattooed, free spirited, chain smoker who could smoke you out and suck you down like nobody's business. I was attracted to her rebellious spirit. She was the last sex partner that I had the chance of encountering and this poem was inspired by her.

Your love brings me to a sensual high. As powerful as my first inhale from tasting your Purple Haze.

As sweet as a grape Swisher, your body is my greatest craze. I inhale your energy and intake your juices.

One hit has me buzzed. You drive me wild with your talents. You keep me on cloud nine.

The best thing about this sex high is that it's never ending. You're all mine.

I love hitting this sexual chronic. You're so addicting that I have to take more than one puff.

As my lips wet your tip, I realize that I'm under your control and I can't get enough.

As I take in your cloud of smoke, you become stronger.

And I begin to choke, you're now inside of me, and I'm as high as can be.

This is better than any doobie any sales man could provide to me.

I feel like I'm floating on your stems.

I'm floating off of your power.

I'm high, eyes red, and I'm craving you again every hour.

You have me feeling some type of way off of your gas.

Your strength knocks me to my ass, but I love it.

You're my kind of high. I'm buzzed off of you. This is a strong sexual high.

I felt my dick begin to swell up and rise inside of my slacks as I finished that poem and I recollected on her being on top of my hands pressed against her hips. A feeling of seductive nostalgia spread across my body like cream as I envisioned Kassidy's toes being in my mouth as I slowly fucked her senseless with her feet pressed against my tight pecs. I closed my eyes to hear her moans again, to feel her touch again. I was going to miss Kassidy, she was a good way to say goodbye to the ATL.

My biggest problem was that I had a hard time falling for anyone on the real tip. Sure, I had the occasional romp that turned into a relationship, but it never really lasted long. As quickly as I could bring a woman home, I could call them an Uber and never see them again with the exact same speed. I have never fallen in love, I have never had a relationship that lasted longer than six months, and at this rate I had no dreams of prospering anything into marriage.

Most women couldn't handle me sexually so how they could possibly handle me in a full-blown marriage?

What was marriage anyway? Some verbal contract signed that guaranteed that everything you have had to be split with someone else? Naw, I'll pass. I had no interest in that. I only wanted the *mo betta*. If I could get my dick wet and keep my wallet heavy, I'd be a happy man. At least I was honest about it, no matter what woman I had in my sheets, I made sure to tell them that it was about nothing but sex.

That way, my tires don't get slashed, my windows don't get broken, and my house doesn't get the Left Eye Lopez treatment. I closed my laptop and placed my hands behind my head while imagining what the L.A. women would be like. Hopefully I could find one that could match my insatiable sex drive. Lord knows that was easier said than done though. The best thing about moving to a new city was that nobody knew me and what I was capable of. A fresh start was always so nice.

All I knew was that my best friend Khali was waiting for me to get there so that he could help me move my stuff into my loft. Khali had been my homeboy since junior high. He was damn near my brother at this rate. Even though we lived in different cities, I always kept contact with him and now that I was moving to his "Kingdom" as he called it, we could cause some trouble like the old days.

Khali was just as talented as I was with poetry, hell he was even better because he had actually made a living off of his poetry and his paintings. Not only did Khali win lots of money winning poetry slam competitions, but he also had a very lucrative YouTube channel that had millions of views and subscribers. He also was a talented and I mean talented painter who could illustrate the world itself with no issue. The entire reason that he moved to L.A. in the first place was so that he could find his niche, which he did, so I was proud of him. It was nice to see Khali getting paid doing what he loved. That man had a mind that could help shape the world into a more positive place to live.

Right as I considered writing another poem, the plane finally took off and I was then joined by another occupant with the sexiest brown sugar skin imaginable. She had a pair of Rose Gold beats across her neck, and she was giving me a soft kiss with the stare that she presented me with.

She was fine like a mix between Mya, and a young Nia Long. I'm talking Nia Long from Love Jones. This girl was a honey drop from the Garden of Hades. I don't know what water she was drinking but I needed a few bottles of it. This woman was exactly what I didn't need to be seeing right now; a vixen, a femme fatale of love that was trouble in a pair of tight black slacks.

"Hello," she said in a soft hush. "My name is Teri. I guess we're going to be sitting next to each other this ride."

"I guess so. My name is Avant. Avant Moore. It's a pleasure to meet you."

"Trust me. The pleasure is all mine," she said with a soft whisper.

We clenched hands and she eyed my work with one eye, while keeping the other one tightly on me.

"You write?" she asked with a high intrigue.

"That's my job. I take pride in it too."

"That's interesting. I've met a few writers where I'm from but not too many that are as fine as you."

"Oh really? And where would that be so I can go and be the main attraction?"

"Brooklyn."

"And what's your purpose in L.A. Ms. Teri?"

Teri then pulled out a notepad before saying, "I'm a real estate agent. I've found some good property in Los Angeles that I plan to sell. I'm guessing that both of us will likely run into each to other. If you ever need a good home, you should give me a call. I can make it worth your while."

"Can you really?" I asked as I felt her warm hand laying firmly across my lap.

"I can. And I will. But only if it's meant to be. I'll let you find me. Now get some sleep Mister Avant. You seem to have some busy times ahead of you."

Teri then placed on her glasses, giving her the look of a seductive librarian as she started reading *Afterburn* by Zane. Teri would every so often turn a page, look at me, and smirk before continuing her reading. It was hard to sleep because I honestly wanted to know what was driving her wild inside of that book.

What was she thinking?

I finally closed my eyes as my dreams were literally up in the air getting ready to take me into another stratosphere.

Until we meet again, Atlanta.

The Next Day

Once my flight landed, Khali's goofy ass was standing with my name written on a piece of cardboard that it looked like he had cut out himself. This dude was dressed as the stereotypical limo driver; hat, glasses, the whole nine yards. I got my stuff and approached him while shaking my head at him.

"What's up my dude?" Khali said as he took off his shades. "Are you Avant Moore the writer?" he asked sarcastically.

"Maybe. Who the hell are you? I mean, you look like my douche of a best friend Khali. I just can't tell with those whack ass dreads attached to that scalp."

"Man, whatever! Bring it in." Khali gave me a hug and slapped me on the back a few times.

"Welcome to the City of Angels my dude. My Kingdom." Khali said as he opened his arms wide.

Khali was a lot shorter than me, five feet eight at the most and he was a bit thinner too. He looked a lot like Ralph Tresvant which I usually gave him shit about but now he was rocking these long dreads to match. I almost didn't recognize him.

"Why are you dressed like that man?" I asked as I looked down at his attire.

Khali said jokingly, "I wanted to make you feel like the world-famous writer that you are."

I waved him off and said dismissively, "Ahh man don't start. I'm not famous."

"But you will be." Khali said as his expression became quite serious. "I have faith in you man. You just made a move that's going to change your life in a more positive direction. I can't wait to see you put your plan to prosperity into motion."

Khali had his goofy moments but for the most part, the guy was a smooth talking cool head who could be a really great person to get advice from. Khali was a lot different than me in that he wasn't as sexually open as I was. Khali was the type that had to be truly rocking with a woman before he put the moves on her. I couldn't knock him for it either.

As we walked from the LAX to Khali's fresh looking red Jeep, I took a big whiff of the Cali air. I couldn't believe that I actually made it here, where stars were made.

"You okay brotha?" Khali asked as he turned around to see me standing still.

"Yeah, I'm just taking it all in."

"Well get used to it my friend. You're going to create some memories here in this bad boy."

Khali grabbed my bags and placed them into the trunk as I entered the passenger side of his ride.

"So, what's the plan for tonight?" I asked as I popped a piece of Winterfresh gum.

Khali made a right turn while responding. "Well, I figured once you got settled into your loft that we could hit the club scene. There are a couple of spots that we could hit. You know, to celebrate your new life here in the Cali sun. That's if you're up for it."

"Man, you know I'm up for it. My loft will still be full of boxes and shit, so I'll probably just check into a hotel for the night since my bed won't even be set up."

"Perfect. It'll give you a chance to see what the women are looking like. I know that's what you're really after."

"You just gonna bust me out like that, huh Khali?"

"I'm not mad at it man. I already know what's on your mind. Trust me, the Cali women are everything. You'll be addicted. Just make sure that addiction doesn't become dangerous. Some of these L.A. women have a tendency to be more of a poison."

"You sound like you're speaking from experience there man."

"I am." Khali said regretfully as he stopped at a red light. "A lot of things have happened since I last seen you dog. A lot of things that I wish I could take back. Some things I wouldn't take back for the world. But let's not focus on that though, tonight is all about celebration. We're going to pop bottles until the sun comes up."

I didn't know who Khali was trying to convince, me or him, but I could tell something was bothering him. I wasn't sure necessarily what it was, but for the moment I wasn't going to interrogate him on it. I was sure when he wanted to say something about it that he would.

Khali took me to my loft and helped me place my bags in with the rest of the boxes that had been moved days before. I was in awe at how dope it looked inside. The loft itself was a two-story beauty with a pool outside and a patio that gave me a great view of the city.

While it was going to take some time to truly get everything set up, I was motivated by at least having it.

"Damn look at this place man. It's too legit for words." I said to Khali as I took in the view.

"Yeah man. You deserve it. You truly do. Well look, I'm going to go home, I have a few things to take care of. But I'll see you later on tonight right?"

"Of course, can't wait."

"Alright. Oh, and Avant…" Khali called out to me as he began to turn around.

"What's up man?"

"I'm glad you're finally here. I'm proud of you. I mean that."

"Thanks, brotha."

Khali then left the loft and left me with all of the baggage that came with me. I began to unpack, first unpacking the box with all of my clothes. I grabbed a few essential things that I could take with me once I checked into my hotel room. I lit a cigar and blew smoke over my patio to enjoy a few moments of civility alone.

The night was only beginning to get started though. I couldn't wait to see what Cali was about to offer me.

Chapter Four

Khali

One Day Prior

"When are you going to let me fuck you Khali?"

Jolani was tired of the games she was as seductive as a street walker on Coney Island and as hungry for lust as a fat kid was for cake. I swatted her hand away as I continued painting my latest piece. *Love for Los Angeles* was what I entitled it. I was painting an entire overview of the Los Angeles skyline and I was almost finished, if only Jolani would have stopped trying to get a bird's eye view of the overview in my joggers.

I swatted her hand away before explaining. "Jolani come on now. You know how I'm rockin. I already told you not until marriage. Chill with it."

"You're making it seem as though we're not going to be hitched or something Khali. You might as well let me test run it baby."

Jolani tried this act so much it was becoming signature for her. This was the main reason that I even practiced celibacy in the first place, was to see if she could handle not having the physical. Whenever I brought up waiting until marriage, she would pull the we're getting married anyway card as if she were just waiting for the ring to be slipped onto her finger any day now.

Truth bc told, I wasn't too sure about Jolani, not just yet, it was just my mind playing tricks on me again. Some days I was rockin' with her, some days I just wanted her to leave me be. Our relationship was truly like a cup of coffee because it was hot and when left unattended it was cold as ice.

Jolani was this cold little number that I met back a year ago when I was still assistant manager at Benny's Pizza. She would come in all the time to grab a super slice of pepperoni and pineapple, but she would always want me to make it for her specifically.

I called her *Jo Angeles* sometimes because when I met her she had this outrageous personality and a heart the size of the city itself. She had everything boy a smile that could stop a heart, the body of an icon, and a roller coaster's kiss, it could leave you breathless.

So, what the hell was wrong with me then? Not for nothing, there really wasn't one as bad to the bone than Jolani, at least not in L.A. I knew that she was committed to me, but something still seemed off, and her aggressive advances for my dick didn't make things any better.

"Marriage doesn't have a timetable Jo-Jo. We still have a lot of work to do on ourselves before I can even consider us ready to walk down the aisle."

"Like what?" Inquired Jo-Jo as she folded her arms impatiently.

"Well for one, I'd like to have an apartment where the fridge isn't rooming with my bed and dresser. Plus, I'd love for one of my paintings to pay off first."

I was living in a tight little loft right in the middle of West L.A. Nothing fancy, nothing too special at all. It was pretty cheap coming I was only paying about five hundred for rent and it was close enough to the main strip of L.A. that I could get to work without much hassle. One day at a time, I was working to create the perfect masterpiece that I could take to the Los Angeles Art Museum for display. I had painted at least six different portraits, but they didn't feel right to me, but *Love for LA* was going to be the one. I was positive that I was going to blow up off this one.

"I swear Khali, you always do this. You make every excuse in the book to escape making love to me. Is this what our relationship is worth? Just staring at each other envisioning what the dick and pussy feel like?"

"Is that all you care about is getting busy Jolani?"

"Is that all you care about are those fuckin' paintings and your fuckin' YouTube channel Khali?"

"Aye, these paintings and my channel are going to pay the bills one day."

"Yeah, maybe." Jolani slipped on her black Vans and threw on her lime green bomber jacket to head out. That was probably her best option.

I stood up with her. "So what, you can't get what you want so you dissin me?"

Jo Jo rolled her eyes and turned back around to face me. "Dissin you? Khali, all I'm saying is that you're the only nucca in Los Angeles that I know that won't give his girl the play. I mean damn, I'm not rockin' any diseases. You know I'm all about you. You know I'm down for whatever, what's the issue? You scared of pussy or something?"

"Wow, really Jolani? You know relationships aren't just about the mo betta. You could see that if you weren't so stuck on me being inside you, you're talking about marriage but not really acting the part of a wife right now. Look at how you're acting."

"So, you really want to wait until marriage Khali?"

"Yes Jolani. I've told you that countless times."

"Whatever dude."

One of the biggest issues with Jolani was that she had a hard time believing that anyone could turn down having a night of passion with her. She was a looker for sure, and I enjoyed the year of mental love making with her, but she was a hot body who couldn't control her urges which turned me off.

No, it wasn't common for men to turn down sex, especially not with someone like Jolani, but I was determined to find someone who wanted more than my dick before giving it to them.

Jolani shrugged her shoulders before adding in, "I'm just saying Khali."

I cut her off. "No, I'm just saying Jolani, if you can't deal with my entire package, then you can't taste my package either. Feel me?"

"You know what Khali?"

"What?"

"I think it's best that I leave. When you're ready to be a man and give me what I want then call me."

"Well, when you're ready to be a woman, and respect my values, I'll try to remember your number. Until then, get to steppin." I held the door open for Jolani, watching her curves sway out of my apartment as I slammed the door shut.

"Fuckin' tramp."

Damn. Jolani just had to prove herself to be just as bad as the others. It's quite a shame too. I really had high hopes for her. As I watched her walk down those bright L.A. streets with her hoodie on, I had to wonder if I had made the best choice for my love life or if I had just given up on my one and only chance for possible matrimony.

One Day Later

I hadn't heard from Jolani since we had that blow up at my place. No phone calls, no letters, not even an occurring run in at Benny's. At this point, I knew that it was truly over. I put my issues to the side though because my homie Avant was new to the city and I didn't want him to see me bugging out. It was definitely bugging me out too.

Maybe I wasn't truly in love with her anyway. A wise man once said to me, "*You only truly fall in love once in a lifetime. There will be lots of infatuation, there will be a lot of lust filled mistakes that causes your heart to break, but in essence, you only fall in love one time in your lifetime.*

If I would've listened to that wise man when I was sixteen, I would've thought twice about dating Lolita. She was sweet as a cavity causing piece of taffy, and as harsh as a Brooklyn wind chill that made me double the amount of socks on my frozen feet. Lolita was the first girl to ever kiss my unsuspecting lips, blistering them with her poisonous lip balm, leaving me motionless right before she kissed my heart with the words no one should hear at sixteen, "I love you."

Two weeks later, Lolita was making sweet, passionate love to my homie in the backseat of his new Corvette that his ma paid for. How did I find out? Well, I found out the same night it happened, which happened to be the same night of our dance.

The dance that I accompanied her to, the same dance that I spent me and my mom's last to buy my first tux for, the same dance that we promised to share our first dance. Yeah, we danced alright, I spent all night with thoughts dancing in my mind as to why it was taking so long for her to return from the bathroom and she was doing *the forbidden dance* on my homie's lap in his backseat.

Shame. Sadly, my troubles were only beginning to whisper in the wind.

If I would've listened to that wise man right after graduation, I probably would've never given Jhene a chance either. Jhene Jalis, light skinned, five feet three, and not for nothing she was damn intelligent. Jhene was the type of girl that you take home to you family and hold her over your head to present around like she was Simba from the Lion King. Jhene was the first girl that I showed my first painting too affectionately titled, *Cali's Finest.* I will never forget that painting; it took me three days to finish it. I just couldn't get the lining right with the blue sky and the sunset. Yet, I was still so elated to present it to her, I just knew even though it wasn't perfect, just like she had done with me, she would accept it because it was hers. Ahh the irony.

In the same three day span that it took me to finish that painting, it took that same amount of time for Jhene to go behind my back, sell my painting to some Coney Island hustler for twenty bucks just to afford some gift to give to her other man, Tre'von. In a sense, I was only her side guy, a brief play thing until Tre'von got his shit together. Not only did Jhene mess around with me, she did something that completely changed my life for good.

Jhene and I had experienced our greatest passion through the creases in the sheets, which resulted in what would have been my first child.

My first son.

My first king.

It wasn't meant to be though. Jhene found out she was pregnant by me and without warning she gave my king up to a doctor with cold prongs in her hands. I never had a chance to see the ultrasound. She was so callous with the way that she killed my son and moved on with her life.

Not for nothing, I never got over that, it was the last time I believed in true love, ever. That was also the day that I had decided to practice a celibacy after having my heartbroken so many times before. The person that I did decide to get busy with in the future would have to have connected with me on a spiritual, mental, and physical level. If any woman could withstand going the distance in the ring with me without getting it in, I would know that I had found the one I'd been looking for.

So, what that meant was…

No sex.

Absolutely no sex.

Positively NO SEX!!

It was hard maintaining that promise to myself at first because as a man, it's quite difficult not to want to explore the body of a gorgeous woman, kissing her all over her body, indulging in her sweetness whenever I wanted to. However, that's exactly why I had to hold off. I wanted my perfect woman to understand that I was looking to make love to her mind first. I wanted my perfect woman to realize that I'm not using her for sexual urges. The problem was that the women that I had professed my promise to in the past either laughed in my face, told me flat out it wasn't going to work, or just got up and walked away. I didn't see what the big problem was with being celibate, maybe they were used to guys being sexual hound dogs, maybe they thought I was gay.

Even when I wanted to find a new woman to chase after, I was usually turned on. For example, I'll never forget the time I had to catch the bus because my car was giving me shit. I had met this woman who STOLE MY SOUL instantly. True story, my body felt obsolete in her presence.

It was a few days before Avant was supposed to fly down. I was sitting on the bus and was about to get off as I felt it come to a stop, the last stop before I'd be home. My eyes remained shut, my mind wandering, my focus on the music calming my soul as I felt something brush against my shoulder. A sweet, almost addicting smell then danced into my nose to awaken me. The smell was alluring that it mystified me in a sense. It was a combination of cocoa butter and vanilla, a very delicious smell.

On the right side of me, the seat that was once unoccupied was now commandeered by the presence of a young lady. With a melanin that could make the midnight sky jealous, an unkempt curly fro that stood up with such personality, it was clear that this woman was a sight to behold. I didn't want to make it so obvious that she gained my attention, but my eyes were locked onto her magnetically, almost kinetically.

My eyes danced around her body, paying close attention to her jet black thigh high boots that wrapped themselves around her tube socks matching in color, accompanied by a black pea coat and black set of earmuffs that struggled to stay around her fro. I was instantly intrigued, almost mesmerized by her beauty. I couldn't stop looking.

She slowly flipped through the pages of Sistah Souljah's, *The Coldest Winter Ever*, with her head cocked to the side and Ray Bans attached to her face, not paying the world any mind. In my mind, this was the perfect woman for me despite the fact that I didn't know anything about her.

How would I know that she was perfect then?

My body told me so. The way this warm feeling came over me. The way that my eyes remained locked onto her frame as she read. The way that my heart pounded out of my chest told me everything I wanted to know. I wanted to say something to her without seeming like a schizo because I'm sure that a preset image on how creepy train passengers are was probably plastered into her mind.

Mentally I had already said hi five times, nonetheless in person I was completely silent. I guess she felt me staring because she looked up. I looked away, she looked back down, and the staring commenced again. This went on for a few minutes before she slammed the book shut and said boldly, "Can I help you my brotha?"

I tried to look away, trying to ignore her question to pretend that she wasn't referring to me when I knew she was. I thought inside, come on man this is your chance, she's talking to you so take advantage of this situation.

The queen then tapped me on my shoulder to confirm she was in fact talking to me asking again. "Can I help you?"

With her hazel eyes focused onto me now, I finally had her full attention. I couldn't mess up this moment I had to make this count for something.

"I'm sorry, I just seen that you were reading The Coldest Winter Ever."

"Yeah, so?" She said coldly.

"It's one of my favorites. Actually it is my favorite. I love Sistah Souljah."

"So, does a million other people. What makes you so special?"

"I never said that I was special."

"Good, because you're not. Stop talking to me."

Welp, that went very well I'd say. The goddess then scooted away from me, turning her body away from me to continue reading. I guess she wasn't fond of making new friends.

"Sorry to bother you." I said humiliated as I lowered my head. It was an everyday struggle that I was used to trying to meet new women. I was used to being treated like that, so I just let that slide. The train came to my stop and I quickly hustled off of it like I had fire under my ass. I took one last look at the girl before I departed. She stayed seated, reading her book not paying me attention.

I guess that wasn't meant to be, I had to suck it up like the shem that I was and take that college place size L.

See, I had no luck. Like I said before, either the women that I wanted would break up with me because of fear that I was gay, or they would avoid me altogether.

My best friend Avant used to ask me flat out if I were gay when we were younger and of course I'd tell him no. I wasn't gay because I chose to actually respect women for more than their bodies. I couldn't just lay down with anybody. I'd rather know for sure that the person that I was laying down with was my spiritual soulmate rather than being a player like my boy Avant was.

Avant had his style and I could respect the fact that he was honest with himself, but damn that man had a new woman everyday it seemed. I was sure now that he was living in California with me that he was going to go crazier than ever before.

After I dropped him off at his new loft, I went back to my apartment and began to work on my art again. I would give Avant time to get himself settled in while I placed myself in my comfort zone. I couldn't seem to focus though, so I decided to take a walk down Hollywood Boulevard to buy some time before I hit the clubs. When you walked down Hollywood Boulevard, you would see some very interesting things.

For example, there was a guy, very grungy in appearance, frail, Caucasian across the platform playing his guitar. He always played the same song, a peaceful melody, nothing too disturbing just something to soothe the other passengers. I coined him *"Guitar God."* He never played for money and if you tried to throw a single chip at him he would throw it back at you and say, "Not for money. Only for love."

At least somebody still believed in love, I wish that I still did. Now don't get me wrong, I loved the idea of love, especially Black love. Anytime I walked down the street, I had these visions of having my soulmate grasping my hand, smiling, locking eyes with me, giving me life as though my body were dehydrated from heartbreak so many times before.

Black love was like a charger into the battery of life. It reenergizes my soul just seeing two very committed beings giving there all to one another, for better or worse, through trials and tribulations, and for the good, bad, and ugly. I used to be this hopeless romantic with the idea of finding a perfect embodiment of Black love. Now I just had no hope, no hope for my own love, no hope for anything really.

I had been living on my own since I was eighteen, right after graduation I took the unconventional approach and got to steppin' mainly because I was feeling my parent's strict rules. When I left from under my parent's thumb, all I had was my sketchbook, my canvas, and a thousand dollars that I saved up from working at Benny's Brickhouse Pizza when I wasn't at school.

Now at the age of twenty-nine, I spent lot of my time doing artwork for the locals on the street. I did caricatures for fifteen chips a face, working on my canvas for entertainment, selling my artwork for a few hundred chips a painting. I was making a decent living, not necessarily living the dream of seeing my art inside The L.A. Arts Museum like I had envisioned, but I was keeping food on my single, marble wood table nonetheless.

I also had my YouTube channel which had 1k followers that would tune in to listen to my poetry. YouTube would pay me for every video I posted, which would always be around four hundred dollars a video and ad. Not too bad. Not too bad at all.

I was usually always alone, just a hopeless romantic looking for love, looking for the next big break. Maybe going to the clubs with Avant would help me find some luck with the ladies. He was always so smooth. I was usually just sitting in the corner with a beer praying for it to be over quickly, so I could get back home to my work.

I was sure that tonight would be no exception. I'd be the wing man with no game and he'd be banging some chick he met by the bar. Yup, I was sure that this life was going to be just full of excitement, I was positive of it. I know I sound cynical but hey, at least he was here with me. I was sure that L.A. could treat him a lot better than Atlanta could.

At least one of us would get some type of thrill out of the night. I figured since he was new in town that he could bring in his new success by getting wild on the dance floor while in the company of some beautiful queen that was implored by his mystery.

No matter what happened later on, it was going to be very interesting.

I was sure of it.

Part 3

Getting

Buck Wild

Chapter Five

Philly

Club Joi was packed to capacity, but we were lucky enough to get in. I was positive that it was because all me and Parker were both looking quite ravishing. We scooted past a bunch of sweaty men who were dry humping a couple of women by the entrance, trying not to rub skin with anybody.

The club was jumping something fierce. *TLC*'s, *No Scrubs* was blasting which gave me such a nostalgic feel that I couldn't help but bob my head.

Parker, meanwhile, was pretty uncomfortable. I could see the look on her face that she really didn't want to be there. The only reason she probably came out in the first place was because I pushed her into it.

"You okay girl?" I asked as we tried to struggle our way to the bar. There were so many niggas trying to hover over us that we felt like the newest additions to a buffet.

"Yeah, I'm just hot. You sure you don't want to try somewhere else?" she said with a slight scowl.

"Nah boo, this place is bumping. This is our spot we're like local celebs in here. It's going to be okay, I promise. You just need a drink or two in you."

"More like a prayer." She said under her breath.

I signaled to the bartender, Amos, to come over to us. Amos was a cool little youngin, 26, sexy, tall, and suave. We banged a couple of times in the past in my younger years. While he had a lot of endurance he wasn't too skilled with the seven inches that he was blessed with. I mean his tongue game was pretty good, his tongue could curve and hit this one spot that made my blood flow like a river.

"What's going on ladies. Long time no see. What can I get for you?"

"The usual for me Amos. A Sex On The Beach, add a lime. I want the sex to be gritty this time the way I like it." I knew if I said that line, Amos would get a hard on in his jeans and would probably reduce the price.

"Coming right up Philly. And what can I get for you Parker?"

Parker rather meekly answered back, "Um, just a gin and tonic. I'm not really feeling this vibe right now."

Amos nodded and walked to the register while I pinched Parker on her arm. Parker used to be such a party animal like myself. I guess that part of her was starting to fade away like a distant fog.

"Girl what is your issue? You see how many men are in here? You should be jumping up with joy right now."

"Why Philly? These men all look like dogs."

"How would you know that simply by looking at them?"

"Ugh, I can just smell the kibbles and bits bouncing off them. I don't see how you can be so excited about going home with one of these men."

"Who said anything about going home with…"

Parker then placed a hand up to my face. "Philly save it. I know why I'm here. I'm here to hold your shit while you get busy with some hairy chested negro in the bathroom stall. You're a nympho. You have sex all the time with some unsuspecting bar patron. It's been your bread and butter since college. Look, next time just leave me at home."

"Parker really?"

Parker went back to the bar, grabbed her drink, and sat by the staging area of the club with her head low. I guess I really must've hurt her feelings. She wasn't feeling me or the night itself at all.

I walked over and grabbed my Sex On The Beach with a sudden urge to leave. If my best friend wasn't feeling the night, then there was no point in being here. I sat at the bar to enjoy what would probably be the only drink that I would be having as every now and then I would watch Parker to make sure she was good by the stage.

"Fuck my life dude." I said to myself as I chewed at my lime. I felt bad because I didn't want Parker feeling like I was using her. I truly just wanted to have a good time. It would be wrong for me to say that I was going to have a good time for her because we came as a package deal.

As I shamefully asked for another drink, the seat that was originally empty next to me was now occupied by another patron. The smell of his impulsive cologne however was overpowering. It had this mystical control over me that made me want to rip his clothes off without even looking at him. There was nothing sexier than a good smelling man, and this man smelled like Heaven.

I could only feel his presence. I could only feel his stare as his deep voice got the attention of Amos the bartender. "Sex on the Beach for me."

I looked up from my drink and we both locked eyes at the same time. I gave him a quick smile, nothing too flirtatious but a smile that told him that I was glad that he decided to join me by the bar. I instantly gave him the Philly test of approval by checking him out. This man was perfect, his fingernails were well trimmed which meant he likely got manicures, which meant that he knew how to take care of himself. His lips were juicy and soft looking. I bet he knew how to use them too.

His middle finger was longer than his others which usually meant that the dick was going to be at a satisfying length. *Yup, this guy passed the test.*

With a gold Rolex that fit his wrist so snug, a tight black shirt that made his already muscular frame pop before my eyes, and a gold chain that was wrapped so beautifully around his neck, I was star struck.

I had just met this man, but I wanted to glide my pussy lips across his beard that looked like it felt like pillows. I wanted to rub my hands across his broad shoulders, and I wanted to lick his face because it looked like it tasted like honey. This man was the personification of handsome. It was like things were going in slow motion as he sipped his Sex On The Beach. I shamefully watched the liquor slide into his mouth, as his lips sucked the juices and licked the rim of the glass.

I looked back down at my drink again and then turned to see that Parker was now joined by a gentleman with dreads. I was hoping that he was making her night a bit better than it started.

Meanwhile, the smell, the look, and the swag of this mysterious stranger was making me want to get to know him. I had to say something, well.... maybe.

Chapter Six

Parker

I was so ready to leave. My heels were practically racing me to the door. I was so over this club scene already and we had literally just gotten there. I sat by the staging area to stay away from Philly. I didn't want to say the wrong thing to her because I really did love her. I just wanted her to see that she was getting too old to still be going to clubs chasing after pussy hungry scoundrels with no conscience attached to their pathetic souls.

I threw back the last of my drink and threw my cup away. At least I thought I did, my cup went nowhere near the trash can. Instead it hit the innocent feet of a lone wolf standing by the wall. The ice made him jump as he kicked away a few pieces, and his eyes danced near my direction.

I was immediately entrapped into his vision. His focus was completely on me and the feeling was mutual. Now, I usually wouldn't play the staring game with me because it was adolescent behavior, but this king was quite the specimen. With long dreads that were black as midnight at the top and burnt orange at the tips, I was fascinated by his unique aura.

The man seemed to be comfortable being his own company. He stood idly by on the wall with one foot pasted across it like some type of smooth criminal. This was the type of guy that I liked; mysterious, the loner, the silent assassin of seduction with no rush of chasing after what he wanted.

I mouthed the words "sorry" at him and he nodded his forgiveness at me. Maybe he wasn't looking at me, maybe his focus was another chick, and me throwing my cup at him simply threw him off.

Well that's what I thought until he started approaching me as my breaths became a rapid succession of skips. My heart was racing like an Olympic game and once he sat next to me, I was beginning to mentally panic. I felt like the girl in school who never got the guy until the guy came to get her. I felt like the ugly duckling who had finally scored the prom date out of pity. This handsome stranger was more than fine, he was the glass of wine that you know you shouldn't have but you have it because it relaxes you after a long day.

Musiq Soulchild's *Ridiculous* began to play and suddenly I had the urge to bob my head like I was really feeling the tempo. I was really trying to play cool so that he would think I was having a good time. *I was a hot damn mess.*

The guy pointed to his shoe and said jokingly, "You know I just bought these loafers, right?"

I leaned back and gave him that *oh hell naw* look, "Um. I said sorry sir."

A shy smile crept across his face and he said, "I'm just playing. I just wanted confirmation that's all."

"Confirmation of?"

"Confirmation that your voice was as sweet as I envisioned it to be."

I won't lie, he caught me with that line and my heavy blush told him so. I allowed him to sit closer to me as he extended his hand to me, "The name's Khali. Khali Carter."

I observed him, he looked so familiar to me. I didn't know if it were because I had seen him in public before or in my dreams. Something about him felt so familiar, he was a human déjà vu.

We shook hands; his hand was so warm, and so tender that I wanted to take it home with me.

I said to him with a smile, "Nice to meet you Mr. Khali. I feel like I've seen you before."

"That's because you have." He said with a strong confirmation.

"Oh yeah?"

"Yeah, I was the dude on the bus that one day way back. You were reading the *Coldest Winter Ever*, and I was trying to be your friend. You were mean as a substitute teacher that day."

THAT WAS IT. I knew I had seen this guy before. I thought back to the day that I was sitting on the bus because my car had stopped on me the day before. I was having such a bad day, my boss was being a douche, my feet were hurting, and my mind was racing about. This guy came up trying to smooth talk his way into my heart and I was so full of impatience I cut him off. I had regret; I went thinking that I might have potentially dissed my future husband. Now here he was, sitting in my face still giving me attention.

"No way that was you."

"Yes, it was."

"You for real? You remember that?"

"I remember it because I never forgot it or you. It's funny that we're here tonight. You yelled at me that day, and now tonight you're throwing drinks at me."

I let out a soft giggle. "Um. Yes. It is every funny. Very funny indeed. Look, I'm very sorry about that day and about the whole drink thing. I've been having a bad night."

"Already, it just started."

"Yeah, well it's common place for me you know? I always seem to have the worst of days. I'm like a walking dark cloud. Things look up one day and then the next they're staring at me as I'm sprawled on the ground hopeless. I'm Parker by the way."

"Nice to meet you Parker. I'm sorry to hear that you're having a bad night."

"Yeah don't mention it. I seem to have a lot of those these days."

"Well, maybe meeting me will alleviate your bad days and turn them into the days of bliss."

I gave Khali a look before saying, "Oh, so you just gone try to slide in like that huh? Who are you supposed to be? Mr. Smooth?"

Khali looked around before adding in, "No. I'm a lot like you. I'm often hopeless. A hopeless soul looking for a common place. Meeting you again, as whacky as it was, actually gave me hope."

"Hope for?"

"Hope that life actually blesses you with second chances. You want to step out to the patio area? It's getting kind of loud in here."

I thought about it for a moment. On the surface Khali didn't seem like a freak or creep, his words flowed from his tongue like vanilla cream, so I wanted to give him a shot. I felt like he deserved it after being cut off the first time we met. I nodded and allowed him to grab my hand as we dipped out to the club's little patio area where others were sitting with their drinks.

The atmosphere was hectic, but we found a spot to sit where nobody would be all in our grill.

"So, Ms. Parker, what is it that brought you out to Club Joi when you don't seem to be in much of a joyful mood."

"My best friend Philly wanted to come out. I'm not much of a party animal the way that she is. I'd rather be at home painting."

Khali's eyebrows perked up as did his interest.

"Oh so you're a painter?"

"Yeah. It's my first love. Painting takes away the pain and…"

"Creates a pleasure from within." He cut me off by saying.

"Oh, so I'm guessing you're familiar with art too?"

"I am." Khali said as he pulled out his phone and showed me one of his pieces.

"I paint but I'd say I'm more diverse with my poetry. I don't know if you've ever seen my YouTube videos but it's how I've pretty much made my living. I perform down at the Soul Lounge every Friday night. You should come and check me out."

Khali's entire vibe was one that captivated me because behind his sexy, squinted eyes was someone who probably had a few skeletons that he was hiding. I wanted to know more about him, I wanted to explore him.

"So, Khali, do you always stand in clubs waiting for women like me to come along so we can throw ice at your shoe?"

After a slightly uncomfortable laugh, he said to me, "Not really. My homeboy Avant just moved here from Atlanta. I was showing him a good time even though I'm sure he's probably by the bar doing a good job of that himself."

"Well, maybe you should go find him. He's probably looking for you."

"He's good. Besides, I'm having more fun getting to know you. I'm hoping the feeling is mutual."

I didn't want to seem so obvious, but I was highly attracted to Khali. Not just because he was the first guy to approach me, but because he approached in a way that I wasn't used to. I wanted this night to go into eternity so that this moment would stand till the end of time with us.

I then asked, "If I said that I was having a great time what would you say?"

Khali said then, "I think that I would say that I hope to continue making your night one that you can remember."

I quickly changed the subject on him as our eyes began to play a chess game with one another, "So Khali, how about you give me a preview of your poetry."

"Right now?" Khali said elated that I sought investment in his craft.

"Yes, right now. What you got?"

Khali cleared his throat and scooted closer so that I could hear him.

Say baby can I be the dawning of your midnight ecstasy?

As our skin bathes in the ebony glaze inside my room, our bodies covered in perspiration, heated by the smoldering fires inside of our hearts.

Allow me to indulge in the sweetness of your cocoa butter skin as my lips dance from your neck to your delicious, pretty polished toes.

As we hide in the secrecy of the sheets, buried in the entrenches of our secluded seduction, you and I create something magical.

Inside of you, I whisper into your ear my dedication to your existence.

You ride me so fluently. Your maple brown taste is heart racing.

Your love making is so powerful, addicting, mystifying and exhilarating.

As you lay across my chest, I lay soft kisses across your forehead that numbs your spine.

It is during this night that my dreams of making you mine becoming concrete.

Five minutes until dawn.

The fears and doubts that we both entered with are gone.

Evaporated in the sky as the moon and stars dance without care you look deeply into my eyes with your hazel brown glare.

And I run my fingers deeply into your soft, silky hair.

The clock strikes 12 and we jump into another round.

I kiss methodically from your left thigh to your right with a musical overtone. Like the greatest R&B song you moan only to my ears.

And once again we hide underneath the sheets, nothing could ever take away this feeling, it's a soul snatching orgasmic feel that leaves my body in a vegetative state.

Damn near obsolete.

This is the greatest midnight ecstasy.

This is what you do to me.

Khali's words stole my soul and placed it in a hypnotic capsule; I had no words initially for how talented this man was. Virginity or not, this man just made love to my senses with his words.

"So, what did you think?"

"I think that I want to know what part of Heaven you came from so that I can send you back. You don't belong here with us normal people."

Our collective laughter did something to my soul. It had been so long since a man could truly make me laugh. I had forgotten why I was mad in the first place in his presence. He was that good at taking my mind away from the negatives. If I had a dollar for every time that I met someone who could make me laugh, I'd have a dollar to tip the bartender with.

We sat on the patio continuing to talk until the night became young it seemed, and we shared amongst each other our greatest fears, favorite artists, and even our birthdays. I found out that he was a *Taurus*, a very calm one at that which explained the attraction to my *Cancer* soul. It was safe to say that Khali was leaving quite an impression on me within our short time together so far.

Chapter Seven

Avant

The DJ had just begun playing one of my favorite jams, *Ms. Philadelphia* by Musiq Soulchild when I noticed little mama next to me giving me eye action.

Honey was straight checking for me. I could see by her side eye from the side of me. I would turn to her and she would turn her head the opposite way. I knew it from the body language she presented to me that she was digging me and I must admit I was checking for her too.

I finally sparked up the nerve to say to her with confidence, "May I ask you a question little lady?"

She looked up at me with a sudden relief that I had said something to her. Mama was badder than a three-year-old with a caramel complexion that brought a sudden adrenaline rush to my pores and a waist that was out of this world. Her face gave off the vibes of Keri Hilson, and she smelled so sweet I could've devoured her whole.

"Maybe, it depends on how good the question is." She answered with a devious glare.

"Are we going to keep staring each other down or make a move?"

She was instantly caught off guard by my bold appeal. "Wow. That blunt huh?"

"Yeah, it's the only way that I can truly be. I see you checking for me…"

The woman placed a hand up and said, "Whoa. Let's get one thing straight big daddy, you were checking for me. I could feel you staring from a mile away and you're sitting right next to me."

"Oh, is that right?"

"It's damn right."

"Well let's say that I was checking for you. What would you do about it?"

She was devilish in nature, the way that she glared in the abyss of my soul and made me feel her body from within. The way her nipples were protruding already through her tight black dress and the way she licked the rim of her glass to tempt me.

Who was this woman?

"Is this the type of question that's supposed to be answered verbally or physically?"

"Your choice. Choose wisely," she said as she took a lime and sucked on its meat.

"What's your name sweet lady?"

She cocked her head and said, "Philly. Philly Washington."

"Hmm, like the song describes. Ms. Philadelphia. And I'm guessing you grew up on the west side as well?"

"Maybe. Maybe not. Look man, why are we playing this introduction game? You're obviously concerned with more than my name correct?"

"You're pretty blunt yourself my Queen."

"I have to be. There are two things that I don't like to waste in life. A glass of liquor and time. I'm already full of liquor so let's not waste any more time."

I asked her cautiously, "You don't even want to know my name?"

She then shut me down with a simple, "No."

"Why is that?"

"Because you know mine. And if I like what I get, maybe I'll want to know yours."

This woman was serious, like a death sentence, and her sex drive was higher than a roller coaster. I thought that I loved sex, but I guess I had just met my match. I decided to not waste any more time with her. I slipped her the address to my hotel and said to her vivacious face, "If time is your best friend, bring the both of you to my hotel tonight."

Philly stood up with the card that I had given to her and said, "If you're lucky. Only if you're lucky."

Philly then walked with a sexy swagger to the dance floor right as Sean Paul's *Give It Up to Me* began to shimmer over the loud speakers.

Chapter Eight

Philly

I sauntered over to the dance floor while waving my new little handsome stranger over to me. The way that I rocked my hips to the music with a sexual prowess lured him to me, and he walked behind as I grinded across his hips to the beat of the music. I made it my duty to make sure that my ass was pressed against his dick to make him rock hard.

His strong, mighty hands were pasted against my hip as the music plus the alcohol were bringing out the freaky side in me. I placed a hand across the back of his neck while we bounced amongst the rhythm. I was feeling the vibe that this setting was bringing forth. I was turned on, I couldn't lie.

I really wanted to see two things through this experience. I wanted to see how on point his rhythm was, and if he could handle my limber body through the music because a man that can dance is a man that can fuck. The warmth from his body rose my insatiable appetite for loving, his grip on my body made me want to take him down right on the dance floor, my pussy was thumping like a rabbit's heartbeat.

I twisted around so that I could face him as now we were staring into each other's souls and my left leg was elevated by his arm. Handsome guy dipped me before bringing me back up and I then teased him with a curl of my tongue across his bottom lip. I watched his reaction change, the breaths in his body become heavier and his desire to kiss me became evident.

I wouldn't let him win so easily though, I pushed him away before jumping into his arms. I lowered my face near his and right before I pecked him on the lips, the song ended which made me hop down. I waved the card that he gave me across my chest and then slowly walked away from him, leaving him on the dance floor to prosper what could be next.

If only he knew what I had planned for him, he'd been prepared for the best of what I had to offer.

Chapter Nine

Parker

I was having the time of my life with Khali, more fun than I had in a very long time with any other man. I was enjoying riding the vibrations that his heartstrings were providing to me as we danced closed to one another. The way that we strolled in a meticulous rhythm made my body turn warmer than the thermostat in the winter time.

As the song switched, our chemistry remained strong and radiant. I was feeling this dude. I mean, at least the vibe that he presented to me didn't send off creep vibes. So I had no reason to fear him. We stood idly on the dance floor as I looked around for my girl Philly, she was nowhere in sight though which made me worry.

"What's the matter beautiful?" Khali asked as he noticed my worry setting in.

"I can't find my home girl."

"Maybe you should call her."

I tried to call her, but I got no answer. I looked around the club which was difficult with all of the bodies piling on one another like a mosh pit. Philly was a big girl who could take care of herself, but she was still my best friend who shouldn't be left in a club alone.

Right as I was about to start truly freaking out, I then noticed Philly starting to come my way from the opposite end of the club. I don't know how I didn't notice her before. I was glad that she was okay nonetheless though.

"Hey girl. I've been looking for you." She said with an exhausted tone, she obviously had more than one drink.

"You good Philly? You look like you're having quite a good time. Do I need to drive?"

"Girl I'm fine. I promise. You ready to go?" Philly seemed to be in a rush as she asked that question.

I looked back at Khali who had been giving me a wonderful night of bliss. I wasn't ready to leave his side at all. We had gotten to know a lot about one another in such a short time, I felt this strange connection to him.

I reluctantly answered back, "I guess so girl. Come on."

I turned back to look at Khali before slowly walking with Philly. Suddenly I heard Khali scream as he walked behind us, "Parker?!"

"Yes?" I answered as I turned back around to see him with his arms open wide.

"Can I see you again?"

I looked him deeply into his eyes before giving him the only answer that I thought was appropriate at that time, "If it's meant to be you will. Bye Khali."

Truth be told, I probably should've given him my number right then and there, but I wanted to leave it up to God. If I were truly meant to see him again, I would see him no questions asked. If it were meant to be, Khali would be in my crosshairs again.

Once me and Philly got to the car she asked me, "Girl who was that fine little specimen that you were dancing with over there? You two looked mighty comfortable."

I giggled a bit before answering, "It was nothing girl, just a fella I met by the stage."

Philly smirked and replied, "Mhm. Naw, I don't believe that. He seemed to be just as smitten with you as you were with him. I was watching, I mean I was kind of busy myself, but I was watching. So, does this fella have a name?"

"Yep." I said as I looked out of the window.

"Well, what is it?"

As I recollected back to the sweet poem Khali recited for me, I simply answered back to Philly, "My future."

Once Philly dropped me off at home, I laid across the bed as I visualized Khali lying next to me. I put on some Jill Scott as I took a hot shower, allowing the warm mist to relax my body as my mind remained focused on that sexy poetic stranger. I needed to see him again, I had too... it was a must.

Chapter Ten

Avant

She wasn't coming, I was sure that she wasn't coming. The clock stuck three AM and I was unable to sleep after my shower because my mind was penetrated by the presence of Ms. Philly from the west side. The way that our night at the club went, I was trying not to let it consume my mind but it was. I could still smell her, I could still feel her, and I could practically taste her.

I paced around my room with a hunger for her body, and a need to experience the warmth that resonated inside of her. I should've done more. I should've taken advantage of the situation and left her with a memory that would force her to want to experience more of me.

I had given up on possibly having a one night stand with her because it was the crack of dawn and I knew that she was probably already sleeping off her wild night.

Damn.

Now here I was sitting with an extreme boner protruding from my boxers as I laid in bed shirtless and barefoot smelling of the hotel's soap. In my mind I continued to replay every moment that occurred as if it were a TV show, and this time I added in things that I should've said. We've all had those moments when we go back to a situation and begin to punish ourselves for not doing as much as we should've.

Maybe I should've done more.

Maybe I should've said more.

Maybe, I should've been more aggressive.

Whatever the reason, I couldn't sleep so I went out to the hotel's patio to smoke one of my cigars, taking in the view of L.A. that I was blessed with having. Now I thought that I had heard a knock on the door initially, but I was in such a relaxed state that I thought it was my subconscious playing tricks on me.

But then I heard it again, and this time I walked over to the door with a sense of urgency.

I felt like it could've been a hotel attendant trying to check on me, and seemed appropriate because it was almost time for the wake-up call hours. I took a deep breath and put out my cigar before answering the door.

It was her.

Philly.

Philly was standing with her body slanted across the door, and her eyes were locked solely on me like a piece of meat. I thought that I was dreaming, maybe, I mean this woman's beauty seemed like a fantasy. Yet, here she was in all of her glory standing before me in my hotel room.

"Can I come in or should I just stand here?" Philly asked with a trouble making smile across her face.

I grabbed her by the hand and allowed her in as I closed the door, first slipping a DO Not Disturb sign across the door knob. My dick was already doing jumping jacks inside of my boxers it was hard to hide it. I watched Philly walk around the hotel room and nod her head, "Four Seasons. Impressive."

"How so?" I asked to her as she removed her shoes.

"Just saying, you have a good taste."

"Well obviously because you're in here." I said to make her blush. I was successful with that.

"Good answer," she said with a smile. "You mind if I step into your bathroom for a second?"

"No go right ahead." I said as I tried to maintain my composure while seeing her in her skin tight black dress yet again.

Philly glared at me as she skipped to the bathroom, never taking her eyes off my rock hard dick that was trying to say hello to her from inside of my boxers. She closed the door as I danced around a bit, throwing playful punches at the air with an ugly ass smile growing across my grill.

"You know, I wasn't planning to show up here tonight." She yelled from the bathroom.

"Oh really?" I asked. "Well why did you?"

"Because, I realized that I never got your name."

"That's because you didn't want it." I said back.

"Not true. I just wanted to wait."

"Wait until…" I said.

Philly then walked out of the bathroom wearing nothing but lingerie. Her hair was down to her shoulders. Philly's ass was a gift from the Heavens, calling her thick was an understatement. Her body was a beautifully seductive temple, with tattoos covering her right leg with one that stretched to her left collarbone.

"I wanted to wait until I had you to myself for the night. So, can I have you to myself tonight?"

"The choice is yours." I said challenging her to make a move in this sultry game of human chess.

Philly placed her right hand across my chest, her warm fingers maneuvered around my pecs flirtatiously. Philly walked around me as I stood still as her hand led itself from my pecs to my shoulders. I felt her kiss the top of my broad shoulders before leading her lips up the corner of my neck.

My body began to grow hotter as she faced me once again, kissing me softly, and leaving the taste of strawberries across my lips. We stood in the middle of the room chasing each other's tongues with my hands trailing from her waist to around her soft ass. I gripped on her ass tightly. She let out a soft moan to show off her growing enticement and her nipples shivered in the air.

Philly then took her angelic tongue, first curling it across the side of my neck, and then licking a trail down from my chest to my belly button. The way that she would watch me as she teased me made the bulge in my boxers grow to maximum levels. I watched as she started to rub on my dick slowly like a genie rubs a bottle. The room was becoming hotter than the devil's tongue. The temperature was rising as she pushed me onto the bed.

The beauteous Philly then kneeled onto the edge of the bed as she with her teeth pulled my boxers off of me completely. Now, I laid on the bed naked, dick standing full salute and her hands wrapped around it to make me squirm around the bed with goosebumps covering my arms. She vivaciously jagged my dick, focusing on the nerves at the tip as I waited in anticipation as to what could be next. I chose to enjoy the moment her touch was delicate, yet rough, and simply magical. Philly then kissed around the tip of my swollen dick and took her tongue to lick the slit of it to make my toes curl.

She smiled at my reaction because she knew that she had me at her mercy, she was winning the chess battle by default. Philly then took her tongue down the center of my dick before licking down to my balls where she placed them into her mouth while humming. It was a heavenly experience and my heart skipped a few beats.

Philly wasted no more time with teasing me, she now had my dick at her whim, she placed the tip into her mouth before bringing it further in and sucking down on it. With a magician's precision, she then deep throated my stick while jagging it with her right hand. She spit on it, licked it up, and then sucked on the sides of it to really make me go crazy.

Philly's style was unbelievably divine. She was like an undiscovered porn star.

I grabbed the back of her head with my left hand and then my right, encouraging her to keep going. I was near a quick climax, but she could feel it, stopping to lick up my pre-cum. I felt like an angel in my own orgasmic Heaven by how I was being treated with her mouth game. Every time that I would take a deep breath, she would start and stop again before looking at me with a sinisterly torturous stare.

I hadn't even been inside of her yet and I was already consumed by her ravishing nature in the bedroom. Philly was having fun making my body her personal party, and she showed it with the way that she methodically took care of every inch of my skin.

It was my turn to show her what I was made of. I flipped her onto the sheets back first as I got my first real taste of her honey brown skin. Philly placed a hand up to my face and quickly said, "The balcony. Fuck me there first. I want to be fucked there."

She asked and she would then receive because I carried her out to the hotel's balcony where I undressed her from her lingerie. I knelt down to eat her sweet, delicate pussy from the back as she leaned over the balcony. Philly had a desire to let the entire world know that she was being pleasured by a real king, as she moaned loud enough for the entire neighborhood to hear her.

I sucked each of her pussy lips. I was a fiend for her sugary goodness, as I glided my tongue inside of her walls. I then twirled a finger around her clit while tongue fucking her into a temporary paralysis, giving her a mixture of both pleasure and pain. I knew all of the things to do to make her scream it was such an enjoyable time.

I kissed her pussy, licked it, and then kissed every inch of her skin with a pause before I then stood back up to kiss the back of her neck as I got my dick ready. I massaged her throbbing clit before spreading her legs and entering her to a huge gasp from her.

She arched her back, as I placed a hand on the back of her neck while gliding in and out of her. I wasn't letting up on her either I was coming with a reckless state of mind. Philly threw her ass back as I started to pound her faster and faster to a high pitched shrill from her body. The way that she beckoned me to bang her harder from the back was all of the motivation that I needed.

It felt so good being inside of her, the thrill of having sex with her in a setting that was quite unusual really turned me on.

"Yess, like that. Like that."

She gripped both of my arms and dug deeply into them, the pain actually increased my aggression. As I pumped inside of her, she began to let out a seductive laugh she was loving what was happening to her.

She let out a demanding beckon. "Oh yes! Fuck me, fuck me like that. Just like that. Right there, yes."

I gave her exactly what she wanted from me. I gave the ecstasy that she desired as we stood on that balcony. The 3 AM air relaxed our sweaty bodies. Our blood rose to the maximum level and I then picked her up to bring her to the bed. I threw her down and spread her legs to get a taste of her sweet, creamy pussy. I buried my face between her thighs, as she screamed out her chants of eternal bliss.

I then slid back inside of her succulent walls, her eyes began to roll into the back of her head, as she gripped the sheets tightly. I was showing her that stepping into this hotel room was the best thing that she could've done. She would remember this night for the rest of her existence.

I folded her legs across her chest as I pumped inside of her with the intensity of a Lion in heat. I was almost near my climax. The higher her pitch went, the harder that I would go inside of her in the position that I had her in.

I placed one of her toes inside my mouth as I drilled inside of her which made her legs shake. Her mouth opened wide and her juices squirted across the bed. I felt mine coming as well, legs were becoming looser than spaghetti noodles and the tingling sensation became furious. After I hit my orgasm, I ended up slumping down next to her near comatose body and staring at the ceiling in shock.

This sexual experience was something euphoric. A soul snatching, mind numbing experience that changed the way I looked at sex forever. I leaned in next to her half awake and highly satisfied body while whispering, "My name…is Avant."

I ended up falling asleep shortly after smoking another cigar and drinking a beer. Meanwhile, Philly was sound asleep from the bomb diggity that I had hit her with. I mean this chick was sleeping like Cinderella or something.

Poor girl.

The next morning however, I was the one who ended up waking up in a pool of drool with pillow marks across my face. I sat up from my slumber next to a yellow note that smelled of Philly's perfume. On the note it read.

Dear Mr. Avant,

You and that dick of yours was quite the troublesome pair last night. I must say that you did indeed put it down on me. It's not easy to say that considering that I've had some disappointing affairs in the past. However, you were something quite different. Well, I don't want to ramble on too long, I just wanted to say that it was great meeting you and I wish you the best of luck in your future. You won't be seeing me again and it's probably best that way. On the bright side, I can say without a doubt that you were the best I ever had. Cheers to your next lady, she's going to be a lucky one.

Thanks for the bomb sex. Farewell and welcome to Los Angeles.

Philly

I read that note over three times and it made me grow a larger Kool-Aid smile every time that I read it. I kissed the note, placed it in my bag before taking one last look at the hotel room. Philly gave me one hell of a great welcome to the city.

Chapter Eleven

Khali

My mind was still fixated on the beauty that was Parker. I could still smell her sweet perfume. As I woke up the next morning after us meeting, she was stuck on my mind like a magnet next to steel. I had to do something to get my mind off of her, so I decided to go visit my family that lived in Compton.

Momma Claire was my biggest inspiration, my greatest motivator as well considering the fact that she was a hardnosed, well known lawyer, making big bills to bring home to her and my other two siblings. My father passed away a year earlier from lung cancer and she took both roles under her sleeve with no problem even though she was still in intense pain from his loss. I could feel her pain through her grind, she would never tell me so herself, but she missed my father dearly as did I. She was originally from Queens, New York so she had a no nonsense attitude with us growing up. She would always pop us one if we acted up, her discipline was needed though.

I had this little brother, Kojo, seventeen years old, and cornerback for his school's football team. I was expecting him to step up as the man of the house when I departed. I saw big things in his future he had the intelligence and toughness that matched that of our late father, so I never really worried about him in terms of growth on the Compton streets. My only concern was him following behind the wrong crowd, which he had done in the past.

My little sister Kindness was the literal heartbeat of our family. At sixteen she was already expected to be skipped up to a higher grade because of her grades and her sophisticated way of speaking. I predicted she would be the youngest woman ever to reach college with honors. She never even had a grade lower than an A- on any of her tests or report cards. With a fire in her eyes, long hair always twisted into micros, and her favorite book, *For Colored Girls* always under her arm, she was an amazing example of what Black Girl Magic was all about. I asked her one day when she was five what she wanted to be when she grew up and she said, "The President."

I said back, "Why the President?"

She said while shrugging, "Because I want to prove that Black girls can do anything, even be

President." I loved her like she was my own child, and she was getting so old so fast, before I knew it, she would be in college herself.

I placed my headphones around my neck as I approached the front stoop of their house, taking in the smell of hot food brewing on the inside, as the smell of maple pine from the trees on the side of me lured into my nostrils as well.

One knock on the door later and Momma Claire opened up with a radiant smile, an apron around her waist, and her hair tied up in a knot which told me she was throwing down.

I was most definitely home, especially when smelling the aroma of momma's homemade Brooklyn style gumbo, as spicy as can be.

"Khali? Well look at what the Heights brought back to me," said momma as she placed a hand on her hip, sarcasm beaming off of her mugging face.

"Haha, hey momma. Just thought I'd stop by."

"Mhm, I know your game boy, you smell food and you're here faster than WE Energies after a late payment. Get in here. And where's my painting Khali?" Momma inquired aggressively as she pulled me into the house. Momma would always ask me to bring her a painting because of the hours of labor that she went through with me. I usually brought her a painting that she could hang up in her dining room. Not this time, I was so distracted by what happened with Parker that I couldn't concentrate.

"I didn't any bring any art ma. I'm sorry." I said jokingly.

"My ass. Get on in here boy and I oughta pop you one good for wearing red when you know it's crazy out here." My mother and her Queens accent always made me laugh when she gave me shit. I still loved her for it.

The house never changed, not when I moved and not after the rest of the kids moved. Momma always promised to keep it the way it was when we were youngins to keep the same feel to it. All of our pictures were still hung above the fireplace along with our Christmas stockings that she kept reminding her that we were once as small as her palm.

"So, how's life treating you?" She asked while grabbing a medium sized bowl of gumbo, the spices just made me fall in love. Momma knew the way to my heart better than anyone did.

"It's a pain, I'm managing."

"And the boardwalk?"

"I'm selling, not as much as I could inside a museum, but I'm selling nonetheless."

"Good. It's going to be okay son. Just remember that every struggle as a success story right behind it waiting to peak."

"Yeah, I know momma. I hear ya, it's just hard sometimes grinding to be more than a statistic out here on the streets. Pops wouldn't want to see me cry about it, so I won't, but I will admit sometimes I doubt myself."

"Don't ever let me hear you say that again boy. I didn't raise you to be some quitter. You keep that head raised up. You're a King, and between those hands of yours, is a blessing. And one day that blessing is going to bless the entire world, things take time Khali. Love takes time, education takes time, riches, and growth all take precious time. It may seem like the world is moving past you but in reality, it's running alongside you, waiting for you to make your next move. You are greatness Khali, but the world just doesn't know it yet. We need more strong educated Black men like you out there not causing mischief. You are a reason to celebrate our men, don't give up. Where's my daughter in law?"

"I haven't found her yet ma. Trust me, I'm still looking. Looking very hard."

"Boy, listen. I'm not getting any younger, I want my grandchild."

I laughed before saying, "Okay momma. I promise to bring you one soon."

"Good. Good. Don't make me pop you one."

"No ma'am. I definitely don't want that."

Momma grabbed my hand tightly, kissing them both and then kissing my forehead. I then noticed her expression change drastically, something was truly bothering her.

"And that brings me to your little brother Kojo." Momma said in solemn. Judging from her face, what she was about to tell me was not about to be good at all.

"What's wrong Ma? Is he in trouble or something?"

"Trouble? Kojo is past that Khali. I'm worried about some of these people that Kojo is affiliating himself with out here. Now last week, I got home from work to see some knuckleheaded Negroes on my stoop smoking weed, gambling, and causing a ruckus. Guess who was in the center of it all?"

"Kojo?"

"Damn right it was Kojo, talking about he wasn't doing anything. The boy reeked of weed and everything but the cologne he left out in. Not only that but he's been skipping classes, his grades are slipping, and he's been talking back to me a little too much for my liking. I don't know what's getting into him, but I don't like it at all."

"Maybe he's still feeling the pain from pop's death."

"I don't know Khali. I'm not feeling this at all."

I didn't like seeing momma like this, not one bit. She was our Queen and she had been through too much to be disrespected especially by one of her own. When I see her damn near in tears, it makes me want to cry with her, she didn't deserve to be in pain anymore. I didn't know what was going on with Kojo, but I was going to get down to the bottom of it really quickly before I had to break his ass in half.

"I'm worried about him Khali. I'm worried about his football career, and I'm worried about his education. I need you to talk to your little brother before he ends up either on the bottom of my shoe, or somewhere dead on the streets."

I nodded and said back, "Ma, mark my words, I will talk to him. I'll set him straight."

"Good son, thank you. I feel like you're the only one who can really reach him. This would mean the world to me. I know you're very busy, but I do appreciate you. You're my first born and my King. Get him back on the right track. Now, eat that gumbo before it gets cold. I'm going to get some rest."

Momma walked out of the kitchen and as she did, in came my little sister Kindness. Kindness was wearing her dashiki skirt that I had presented to her after she graduated and was wearing a black Marcus Garvey shirt with it. I loved how socially conscious she was. Of course, wherever Kindness went, she had a book in her hand as well.

"Excuse me little Miss. Brown-With-Her-Crown, you can't say anything to your big brother."

Kindness quickly ran up to hug me, "Khali. Oh my God, I've missed you. Did you hear about Kojo? He's been giving mama all types of trouble."

"I did hear and I'm going to take care of it."

"Okay good. Guess what Khali, I was just nominated as President of Student Government." Kindness said this with so much elation it was adorable. My little sister was making all types of strides, I never had to worry about her.

"Word? Well that's what's up. I'm so proud of you Kindness."

"Thanks, big bro."

"So, Ms. President of Student Government, what will be your first ruling?"

Kindness with a thumb on her chin said back, "More soul food in the cafeteria number one. And number two, we need more African American Literature in our libraries. How they can expect us to learn anything in those self-serving history classes that only feed us a half serving of Black History to fulfill our morale with justification? You know who they taught us about for our so called Black History month? Martin Luther King Jr. All month long. Nobody else. Don't get me wrong I love MLK but what about Rosa, or Marcus Garvey, Medgar Evers, Betty Shabazz, Malcolm X, and Vernon Johns? We need to know that our culture was more than just a preacher. We were more than Panthers, we were also doctors, dentist and athletes you know? We were more than just a march on Washington, we were also a march on education if you're Ruby Bridges, marching into a school full of hate filled whites just to get an education with her crown fully adjusted. You see big brother, my goal is to push a new wave of books like the one I'm reading in order fully educate our class on what we must follow as Black leaders. I know I'm young, but I'm not naïve, these history books are NOT giving us the entire truth. I'm going to stand for something I'm not falling for nothing."

Kindness never ceased to amaze me, she was only seventeen, but she knew so much that I had so much faith in her future.

"Well you keep it up baby girl. You're going places."

"Thanks bro. So, are you still taking me to Coney Island next month?"

"I didn't forget sis, I promise. Even with my last dollar, I'm going to make sure that we go."

"Okay, I'll hold you to that big brother of mine. I'm going to go finish this book now. I just came down for an apple. See you in a bit."

"Hey before you go, where can I find that knuckle head brother of yours? Is he upstairs?"

"No." She replied back. "He's out with Lyric and Ky by the alleyway."

"What the hell is he doing out there? Man this dude." I hugged Kindness, placed my gumbo in a doggy bag, and went out to check on my ignorant little brother in peril.

Kojo's friends were usually not too much trouble especially not his best friend Lyric who was always trying to keep Kojo out of bullshit, but this other guy Ky I knew nothing about. I had to investigate this because I could be onto to why Kojo was giving mom such shit.

"Kojo?" I called out as I approached the alley in a rage. "Hey Kojo?"

After the second time of calling out to him, I could see him and his homies in the cut shooting dice as momma had described him as doing earlier. It was quite a sight to see my little brother that had such a prominent future looking like a fool.

"Hey! Get your rock head ass over now Kojo!" I demanded as I pointed at him.

Kojo looked over at me and then his friends with an embarrassed expression.

"I SAID NOW KOJO! Don't make me say it again."

At that moment Kojo then did as he was told with a huff and a puff. Kojo crossed his arms as he stood in front of me it was almost a challenge of sorts. The only thing keeping me from punching him in his chest right there was that momma probably wouldn't approve.

"You mind explaining to me why you're not in the house doing your homework?"

Kojo sneered back, "I'm out coolin' with the fellas. I'll do it later."

"No, you're going to do it now and I won't hear another word of it."

"Man whatever, you're not my pops, he's dead remember." Kojo said back as he waved me off. This boy was really testing me. I didn't know where he got off acting like that.

I grabbed him by his arm and forcefully swung him back around, "Yeah, I might not be pops but you and I both know that he wouldn't be approving of what you're doing right now. You better get your act together really quick or it's going to be me and you. Hear me?"

Kojo lowered his head with a smug look across his mug, "I guess so man."

Kojo walked back over to his friends, shook their hands good-bye, and then bumped past me on his way back to the house. I didn't understand what Kojo was going through, or what could be bothering him, but I was going to get to the bottom of it before it truly got out of hand. I refused to see my little brother fail out on those cold hard L.A. streets.

After leaving my family in Compton, I headed down to the *Soul Lounge,* I thought that maybe doing a little poetry would help get my mind off of everything. The Soul Lounge was my place to seek a meditative refuge when life was going to crazy for me or when I had a lot on my mind.

Well I definitely had a lot on my mind today and Parker was the main subject. The Soul Lounge had this hypnotic vibe it could draw you in and make you feel like family with the other patrons there. It was more than just a hole in the wall type of joint this place was a poet's palace. I hoped that Parker would one day accept my invitation to come and see me perform.

I placed my jacket on a chair near the stage and nodded at my homeboy Alex who was the hostess. That was our silent sign that I wanted to spit some fire next on the stage. He wrote my name down, and gave me a thumb's up. I went to the bar to order my personal favorite, a Scotch on the rocks. I sat by myself by the bar for a minute before it was time for me to go up to the stage.

My mind was full of Parker, my heart was full of hope, and my head was all over the place like a puzzle. I looked around the lounge and it seemed that everywhere I looked Parker was sitting, smiling at me. Man, I had to get this girl off of my mind I was consumed by her power.

I then heard Alex say over the microphone, "Alright ladies and gentlemen, our next poet is someone near and dear to me. Please welcome my homeboy, my brotha from another mother, cut throat Khali Carter. I walked up to the stage and lowered the mic a bit as I envisioned Parker being in the front row. As I placed my lips close to the mic, I closed my eyes and began.

"This poem is titled, Grip on Me.

My baby, my shawty, you have a grip on me.

I'm tormented by the potent taste of your honey suckle lips.

Your hugs were as warm as a Summer Time's kiss.

I'm enthralled your mythical beauty.

You're my nocturnal bliss.

My baby, my shawty, you have a grip on me.

I'm allured by your coffee skin, as complete as the clock striking 11:59.

I'm drunk off your love because you're finer than the last drop of wine.

The moment our meshed lips tango across the danced floor of seduction,

You had me wishing to rewind time.

Just back to the moment right before your lips locked tightly with mine,

So, I can once again make love to your eyes.

Honey you have a grip on me.

A goddess with the walk of my favorite 90's sitcom, you make me feel like the Freshest Prince on the Streets of Bel-Air.

I'm blessed to be Living Single in your presence.

Your touch entraps me, before releasing my soul into the air.

You enthrall me with your cold stare, as frozen as a box office smash produced by Disney.

Queen you have a grip on me.

As tight as the padlock across a high school locker, I was saved by the bell the moment you chose me to be your king.

My voice can even reach a high pitch but just the thought of seeing you consistently makes me want to sing.

You're like the honey dew to my heart.

The sex on the beach to my lips.

You're super glued to my brain.

You're the forbidden fruit in the Garden of Eden that drove Adam and Eve insane.

You're the sweetest dose of cocaine.

You leave me sprawled across my satin rug.

You're the drug, secret supplier and the just in case plug.

My baby you have a grip on me."

I left the stage to a standing ovation from the crowd and grabbed my jacket to leave. I did what I had to do. I said what I had to say. I hoped that maybe that poem would help me alleviate my feelings for the woman that I had been plaguing my mind since the night prior.

Later that night, I began to write a new poem titled, *Black Queens* when I got a call from an unknown number. Unknown numbers were trouble because I knew they were either bill collectors or some fuck ass that I didn't want to speak to. Here I was thinking about my future when my past kept pulling me by my shirt, I answered my phone with a hint of irritation.

"Hello?"

A sweet but deadly voice responded, "Khali? It's me, Jolani. You mind if we talk?"

I looked back at the phone and said back, "Jo-Jo? What you want girl?"

"Don't be cold blooded Khali. I need to talk to you. It's serious."

I sighed before responding, "What's wrong Jolani? Must be something you're calling me from a random number."

Jolani said back in a shaky voice, "Not over the phone. In person. Meet me at the Phatburger by Comp at eleven. I'm serious. I need you. I miss you. Let's talk."

Before I hung up, I reluctantly said to her, "Fine Jo. I'll see you tomorrow."

Chapter Twelve

Philly

I will never forget the way that Avant's dick felt inside of me, it was a feeling of sensual relaxation that couldn't be mistaken or felt again. By leaving him with the note that I left him with, I was hoping that things between us would leave off on a mysteriously sexy note between us.

Sadly, the fun times were over, and it was back to work for me. I wish I would've thought more about work when I went home to crash in my own bed. I was so caught up in the action that it had slipped my mind that work was at 10 am. The sleep that I had was beyond lovely though. I was in the midst of one of those sleeps that was almost paranormal because it didn't seem like I was still living on earth. The sleep was so good that I woke up with drool on the side of my face and top of my arm. Too bad for me that I ended up over sleeping by thirty minutes.

My alarm had gone off almost five times but because I was still in a stupor from good dick and good liquor, I was slumped. It took my cat lying across my stomach for me to finally get up in a rush. I repeated the phrase, "Fuck" so many times that my neighbors probably thought that I was being fucked again. I hopped out of bed like the sheets were on fire and took a quick shower. I was so behind that I tripped getting out of the tub, almost destroying my knee cap in the process. I guess I learned my lesson on going out the day before I'm supposed to work.

The scorching hot air damn near punched me in my perfectly beat face, it had to be at least 85 degrees. I felt like I was going to melt when my foot hit that pavement. Anthony Hamilton's *Can't Let Go* mellowed me out a bit as I drove in the distance to the job. Since I was already running late anyway, I grabbed an ice cold vanilla Frappe from Starbucks before pulling up to the spot. Once I finally pulled up, I hustled into the building like my ass was on fire.

My office was on the third floor of the building, so it wouldn't take me too long to get there but you know when you're running behind it seems longer. The elevator was just starting to close as I ran to it, so I screamed as loudly as I could. "HOLD THAT ELEVATOR!" to the handsome gentleman who was already on it.

The gentleman quickly grabbed ahold of the two doors so that I could slide my skinny ass in.

"Thanks." I said as I sipped my coffee.

"No problem. You seem to be in a hurry this morning," he said jokingly. Too bad for him I wasn't in too much of a joking mood.

I did however briefly make eye contact with the man and to say that he was FIONE would be like saying wine is good after a long stressful day. Not only was he FIONE he smelled exquisitely scrumptious. I could just look at him and tell he probably tasted like a cookie's and cream bar.

"You're Philly Washington, right?" he said trying to extend the conversation.

"The one and only."

With a wide Kool-Aid smile across his handsome face, he added, "I'm a big fan of your writing. Your column keeps my blood pumping in the morning."

I wanted to ask him, blood pumping to where exactly? But the classy chick in me told me not to; besides, I had stuff to do so I didn't have time to try to mentally molest this chocolate brother on this elevator. Lucky for him.

"Well thank you. I appreciate that." I said back coldly.

"It's actually kind of funny meeting you here."

"Oh yeah?" I said back with my eyes focused on the doors of the elevator.

"Yeah, I've been dying to meet you for months. It's hard to do that when I work a few floors up from you."

I could sense his high level of interest in me. I'm one of those types of people that can sense when a man is burning a hole through me with their eyes. I could sense his eyes taking a detour from my ass to my face. I hoped that he was enjoying what he was seeing. Even though he was attractive, he seemed very odd. The oddest thing about it was that I knew everyone inside of the building, but I had never seen this guy before. I had this strange feeling growing inside of me being around him that I only got when I ate cheese with my lactose pills. It may have just been my hangover that had me feeling like that though.

"What's your name again?" I said curiously.

"Javari. Javari Miles."

"Well, Javari Miles from the fifth floor, I hope that you got a great look at my ass because it's probably the last time you'll see it."

I got off of the elevator quickly as Javari screamed back to me, "Well maybe I'll see you later on."

"Or not." I said back bluntly, dismissing him as I got to my office.

"So, it's like that?"

"Yep. Have a nice day on the fifth floor."

That encounter was weird, and that's coming from a girl who once banged her Uber driver to avoid him charging me. I mean homie was sexy and all that, but he had stalker written all over him. Men at my job usually didn't get more than a hi or bye from me because if there was one thing I didn't like doing, it was bringing my personal escapades to the work place. My momma always told me to never sleep where I eat.

I slid into my office slyly and closed my door where my cousin Janae was waiting for me. The good thing about Janae being my assistant was that she was always on time. The bad thing about Janae being my assistant was that she was always giving me shit when I ran late.

"Good morning slut," she said sarcastically as she sat posted on the edge of my desk. "Aren't we later than a *Backpage* hoe's period today."

I turned around clutching my chest tighter than Redd Foxx in Sanford and Son, "Bitch, you scared the shit out of me."

"Did I really?!" she said as she lowered her slim pair of glasses towards her nose.

"Yes. Shit, it's bad enough there's niggas on the elevator trying to taste me already."

"Girl who."

"I don't know, some dude from the fifth floor. He was cute but seemed off. Anyway, sorry I'm late, I had a bit of trouble getting up this morning."

"And why would that be?" Janae said with a smirk and an interrogative tone to her voice.

"I had a...decent night last night."

"Oh yeah? Just decent? Because you have I just got my back blown out written all over you."

"And you know that how?"

"Cousin, I know you way better than most. Your shoes are on the wrong feet. Your shirt is un-ironed. Your hair still has that frizzy look to it, and you have that look in your eyes like you still can't believe the dick was that good. So, who is he, how big is the peener and does he have a brother?"

Janae totally knew me better than most did. Her crazy ass was like the little sister that I always wanted. Of course, I often found myself trying to compete with her vivacious youth. Janae was only twenty-eight, so she was still in her prime compared to me who felt like I still had something to prove banging all of my suitors. Janae was a bit different than me though, while I had more than one man, Janae had girls and guys on her contact list. For the past three years she had been in this off and on relationship with this girl named Averi. Averi is a sweet girl, kind of muscular to be so short, but she was very pretty and good to Janae.

"Okay, okay. You got me. I met him last night."

Janae quickly cut me off. "Wait hold up, hold up. You met him last night and you already gave him the good-good?"

"Kind of."

"Ooh, girl you're nasty."

"Not nasty. It's just, this dude was different you know? Like, I usually don't give up the goods so fast but last night was something major.

Besides, don't act like you've never taken people home from the bar before. I seem to recall you taking home a guy AND his girlfriend two months ago."

"Yeah, but that was before Averi came home from the army. Now whoever I bring home usually gets fucked by the both of us. But this isn't about me, this is about you. So tell me more about this guy with the good vibe. He must've been good if he had you running late for work."

I almost wet my panties again just thinking about Avant. I flashed back to his touch, his lips, and his stroke before coming back to reality again.

"Girl, he was better than good. He was fucking amazing. I swear that man had me screaming like I was giving birth to triplets. I've never been fucked that way before. His dick was like the first sip of soda after you open the can. Better yet, his dick felt better than the first five minutes in the hot tub are you hearing me?"

Janae then said with a smile, "I'm hearing you girl. It was that magical, huh?"

"Magical? Girl, his dick was like having front row tickets to a Lakers game and you get a bird's eye view of everybody's butts you feel me? His dick was like getting your W2's a day early.

Shit. I'm not hungover because of the alcohol I'm hungover because of his stroke game."

Janae seemed so entertained by my story.

"Damn chile. Well I guess that sums it up. So, he gave you some Dick Quil and laid you out for the count huh? Yeah, I love those nights. Nothing like that deep stroking, sheet gripping, back scratching, sweat, dripping physicality."

After almost busting a gut laughing, I walked over to my desk before replying. "Yeah pretty much, I didn't get home until the crack of dawn fucking with him. I mean this dude had me all on the walls and the floor."

"Well damn, you could've invited a sistah!" She said back in a petty envy.

"I tried to hoe, you didn't answer your phone like usual. I'm guessing that Averi was too busy eating your clit like it was a southern style biscuit."

"Something like that." Janae said with a devious face as she snuck a sip of my coffee and then asked. "So are you going to see him again?"

"Didn't plan on it."

"Why not?"

"Well if you must know, we arranged it that way."

"What way?"

"For us to never see each other again. It makes things more interesting in the bedroom. When you realize that you only have one chance to really impress each other, it makes you really bring what you have to the table."

Janae looked hella confused as I explained the deal to her. She scratched her head and asked, "So that's it? You don't want to see him again ever? Like forever? What happens if you happen to run into him at a burger joint or something?"

"Well, it was meant to be if that happens. But I'm not going to sweat it anymore. We fucked each other senseless and now I can move on with my life. There are more men out there. That's it, that's all? So, to change the subject a bit, did you forward all of my emails?"

"Yes, I did, and I have some sexy info that I think you'll want to know."

"Oh yeah?"

"Yup, there's apparently a new hire starting on the fifth floor today." Janae said excitedly as a huge smile glowed throughout the entire room.

Janae was like the TMZ of our floor. She had all of the dirt and she knew everybody's business. If you wanted to know something, she was sure to tell you.

"And I'm guessing it's a guy based off of how giddy you seem to be about it."

"Girl, you know it's a guy. From what I've heard, he's a hot bag of chips. Something out of a magazine fine. We should sneak up to the fifth floor and take a peek for ourselves."

"Um, no thank you boo. You knock yourself out. I've had enough penis for one day and one night. I just want to sit here and get some work done. Does this new hire have a name?"

"Nobody knows his name except for Cheryl. She's the one who hired him but she's not giving anybody the dirt."

"Well, I guess that means that it wasn't meant for us to know. Maybe the new guy will meet that creepy dude from the elevator. Anyway, gone on and go to work. We have stuff to do and I have to work on my article while trying to edit everybody else's."

"Whatever boss lady. I'll be at my desk, if you need anything."

"Better be."

Janae did a quick little bow and skipped out of my office to go back to her desk while I opened my laptop to try to get to work. The key word was TRY because it didn't seem like I was going to be getting any work done with how much my head was banging at the moment. It felt like somebody was doing the running man inside of my head with Timberland boots on and I could only imagine how much worse it was going to be by the end of the day.

Chapter Thirteen

Avant

Time: 11am

I had only been in Los Angeles for a day or so, and already my time here was something out of an erotic novel. My night with Philly was remarkable, powerful, and strong like a cup of coffee on an early Sunday morning. She was dancing in my mind with the same amount of grace and spirit that she was in the nightclub. As I drove into the parking lot of my new job, she was all that I could really think about. I was surprised that I had gotten any sleep at all after my night with her. I actually slept like a baby. The smile on my face as I sat in my car ready to start my first day as an Essence magazine editor was one that couldn't be removed.

As I got out, I took a deep whiff of the magnificent sunny L.A. air that could turn your body numb. It felt so damn good outside and it felt even better knowing that the night before I was drowning in some of California's finest vagina made it even better. I took a moment to take in the look of the building, in disbelief that I had made it this far in my life before strolling inside.

I felt like a big ass fan, snapping pictures of the inside of the building for my own personal collection and waving at everybody like a fucking idiot. I just couldn't help the fact that I was about to work a six-figure salary job of my dreams and be able to utilize my talents to the best of my abilities. There was a receptionist sitting by herself in the middle of the first floor and once our eyes met, I extended my hand to her. She wasn't bad looking, she was actually very pretty, almost like a spitting image of a young Aaliyah. This young lady had to be at least twenty, maybe a fresh twenty-one, and was a captivating woman.

"Hello. How may I help you today?" she inquired with a high-pitched voice, her plump lips bathing in raspberry lipstick.

"My name is Avant Moore, I'm the newest editor here. I'm guessing that you would know where I can find a Mrs. Cheryl Lewis?"

"Maybe?" she said flirtatiously, her eyes were dancing, and she began to pump her chest out as if she saw something that she liked.

"Only maybe?"

"Nah, I'm just joking. Yeah, I guess I can help you with that. Congrats on getting the position by the way."

"Thanks. I like your perfume is that White Doves?"

She seemed impressed by my knowledge as she turned back around to give me a glance. "As a matter of fact it is. Most men wouldn't know that."

"Well, I'm not most men and most men aren't me."

"I see. I love the confidence," she said back to me. The young lady bit her lip and observed my body like it was her next meal with a subtle nod of her head. Man, what was with these ladies being so attached to me and my charm. It was dangerous to be this fine I guess.

"It's not just confidence. It's reality baby girl."

"Hmm, I think that you're going to fit right in around here."

"Well I hope so. So, do you have a name sweetness?"

"Yes, Shayna."

"Shayna. Hmm, you're named after my favorite rap group. You just became my new best friend Ms. Lady."

Shayna blushed and dialed a number over her phone as her eyes remained posted on my body, "Hey Cheryl, your new hire is here, and he's waiting for you down in the lobby. Yes. Okay I'll let him know."

Shayna hung up the phone and waved me back over to her. "Mrs. Lewis will be down in a second to come lead you to your new office Mr. Moore."

I grabbed her hand, kissed the front of it, and said back, "Baby girl, no need for the misters. I'm not fifty years old. Just call me Avant okay?"

With a glowing smile she nodded and said, "Okay. Avant. It was nice meeting you again. Hopefully, we'll be able to speak more as the month goes on."

I gave her a convincing wink and said, "Oh trust me. You'll be seeing a lot more of me. See you soon Shayna."

I waited for my new boss to arrive as I looked around the lobby, looking at some of the old magazine covers that surrounded me. So many celebrities had graced the cover of Essence, so many black queens, so many stars. I closed my eyes to envision me interviewing someone black and sexy like Taraji P. Henson for an article. I couldn't even get past the first question without me immediately focusing on kissing her until her mouth went numb. I heard the elevator on the right side open up and out came a heavenly body of caramel skin walking towards me in an elegant pants suit. This black queen's hair was draped down to her shoulders, wearing a slim pair of glasses and red lipstick that gave her such a classy look.

The clicking of her heels as she power walked over to me gave her this almost mythical presence that it was hard not to take note of her. I tried not to look too hard at her, but it was excruciatingly tough with how gorgeous she was.

My name exquisitely bounced off of her lips as she patted my shoulder, "Avant Moore?"

"The one and only."

"Well welcome to Essence Magazine. It's nice to finally meet you. I must say after hearing your very calming voice for three weeks, you're definitely as handsome as I envisioned."

"Well, I'm only the appetizer to you and all of your beauty."

After a brief stare down, she led me to elevator, "Here, let's walk and talk."

On the elevator, Cheryl handed me a key and a packet of information. You know the usual stuff, pay wage information, insurance, and other long-winded paperwork that I would probably fill out at the last minute. Cheryl also tried to quiz me on some of my favorite editions of the magazine to which she lost that battle because I knew every edition by heart. I probably impressed her more with the fact that I had so much knowledge of a concept geared towards the sisters.

As we walked to the fifth floor, Cheryl began to show me around. A lot of the other writers seemed to be intrigued by me because I was the new guy and of course the new guy is considered a threat out of the gate.

"I want you to feel as if you're at home whenever you're here Avant," she said while walking me around the floor. "All of our writers are patient and cool so don't be intimidated by any of them. I want you to be brutally honest with them all, don't hold back, tell them how you really feel about their pieces."

"Oh, don't worry Cheryl, I think I'm going to fit right in."

"Good. Well allow me to introduce you to your office." Cheryl grabbed me by the hand and led me to a huge room that was completely dark until she flipped on the light switch. Once she did that, I was in awe at the sight of my own desk, my own Apple computer purchased by the company, and shit even my own coffee maker. I was in love already.

"Dayyum." I exclaimed as I strolled around the lit looking office, taken aback by the space, the lighting, and the privacy. "This is all me?"

"Yep. It's all you." Cheryl answered with a proud smile.

"You're bullshitting me. This is literally my entire office. Like I don't have to share it with anybody?"

"It's all you sweetheart."

"Wow. Man, have I died and went to Heaven already? Sweet Jesus this is a nice office."

"Haha, well I'm glad that it can do you justice. I've been working on it myself all day."

"You're serious?"

"Yes, dead serious. Look Avant, I want you to fit in here like I said before. This job can be consuming, you'll develop a lot of relationships here. Some good, some bad. Overall, you'll be quite surprised at how your life is about to change here at Essence Magazine. But don't fret about anything; I'm here to be your resource. You can call on me for anything, literally anything."

The look she gave when she dropped the *literally anything* part of her speech was quite telling of how I saw our relationship panning out in the future. Especially when I peeped that shorty wasn't wearing a wedding ring on her finger.

"Oh and Avant don't be afraid to explore the entire building. Introduce yourself to some of your colleagues. I'll encourage some of them to come stop in to introduce themselves to you later on. I'm truly happy to have you aboard Avant. I'm sure you'll be a major element here at Essence."

"Thanks Cheryl. I truly appreciate it."

Cheryl slowly closed my door and allowed me to enjoy a bit of alone time with my office. It had the new car smell to it and everything. I just knew that I was going to love it here.

I sat down at my desk, spun around in my chair before putting my feet up on the table like I was a mob boss or something.

"You've made it big fella. You've fucking made it." I said to myself as I let Tupac's

California Love play aloud on my phone as I vibed out in the office. This was my life now, being the big man on campus in an entirely new city. I was loving every minute of it so far too. I couldn't complain.

As I started to truly vibe out, I heard another knock at my door to see a guy standing in the door way. I turned down the music embarrassingly and walked towards the door to the guy. The dude seemed to be giving me a cold, silent death type of stare.

"Sorry about that man. I was in my zone."

His facial expression became phony. A fake smile came across his face as he said, "Nothing wrong with it. I'm a Tupac fan myself, I just wanted to come in and peep out this new guy that Cheryl was praising so highly."

"Yeah man Avant Moo…"

"I know who you are my dude." The guy snapped back. His tone seemed hostile, and antagonistic.

He continued, "I've studied you. Avant Moore. You came from some rinky-dink Atlanta gig. That's nice or whatever but allow me to introduce myself to you because that's what's really important here. My name is Javari Miles.

I've been a part of this company for three years and I'm one of the lead writers here. Don't get in my way, and we won't have any problems got it?"

I had to look at dude like damn, does *Avant Moore have to smack a bitch*? I wasn't feeling that last sentence that he threw at me. I didn't know who the fuck he thought he was talking to. I mean don't get me wrong, I didn't like having to put my hands on anybody, but big homie was talking like he wanted problems. This was only my first day and I was already feeling to choke a nigga like he owed me money.

"What type of problem would that be?" I asked with my fist clenched tightly as I got closer to him.

He brushed off the hostility with a smirk. "Just saying, forewarning. Welcome to the job though. I look forward to working with you Avant."

Javari walked away and left me standing there still trying to figure out what his issue was. I didn't even know homeboy, so I didn't understand how he would have an issue with me. I guess he felt like his spot was in Jeopardy with another guy being on the team. He seemed pretty insecure to me, but that was just my opinion. Hopefully I wouldn't have to bitch slap his ass like Rick James in the future.

Later that day, I decided to take Cheryl's advice and explore the building a bit. The entire structure was so big, that I could've walked around the entire building twice and still had not seen all of it. I felt Presidential, like I was a part of some exclusive club or something. A lot of the other writers looked at me like I was a big piece of fresh meat as I wandered around the building, like a lost child.

One woman saw me standing on the fourth floor peeping some of the old articles on the floor and approached me.

"Hey do you need something sir?" she asked as she placed a hand on my shoulder.

I shook my head no and politely, "Um no. I'm new, my boss Cheryl told me to get to know the building a bit. I work on the fifth floor."

"Ahh. You must be the new editor?"

"Yeah. Avant Moore."

The woman then grabbed my hand and said in return, "Welcome Avant. My name is Yolanda Williams. I'm the main photographer of Essence Magazine. You'll be seeing me a lot. I work on this floor mainly, but I do venture up to the fifth floor a lot too. So hopefully we can see more of each other."

"Well I'm sure we will Ms. Williams."

"Please call me Yolanda. So, is there a Mrs. Moore?"

"Sadly no. I'm a single man."

Yolanda gave me a look of doubt as if she couldn't believe that a guy like me could be single. "Well at this job, that's dangerous. The women here are like vultures looking for a guy like you to snatch up and devour. Just a forewarning, never let this job become your bedroom. Keep your head in the game. One distraction could get you into trouble."

"It sounds like you've seen it all at this place, huh?"

"Oh, trust me, I've definitely seen it all at this place. Everybody here seems to like getting into trouble they can't get themselves out of. But you're in good hands because Cheryl will watch over you and keep you focused. Anyway, enjoy your tour."

"Well I'll keep that in mind Yolanda. Thank you, I'll see you in a bit."

I headed back to the elevator to continue my tour. I decided to go down to the third floor. As I entered the elevator and the doors closed, a strange aura entered my soul. Have you ever gotten the feeling that something was waiting for you on the other side of a door, like maybe a new opportunity, maybe a threat, maybe a blessing in disguise?

Now how would you react if when those doors opened, you saw something staring back at you that made your body tremble a bit? This was a moment that couldn't be paused, or recorded, you had to act accordingly to the situation that presented itself right then and there. Well as the doors opened to the door floor, I found myself in this exact situation.

I was looking down at my phone, scrolling down my Facebook feed, sharing a few posts that Khali had made earlier when I heard the doors open. Now I had a habit of always looking down at the ground, so my eyes were momentarily fixated to the ground when I saw a pair of high heels step in front of them. I looked up to see a pair of the sexiest honey brown legs attached to them. My dick was already doing jumping jacks in my pants looking at these delicious looking legs. The pulse jumping smell of perfume entered the elevator next and as my eyes ventured up, I saw a sight that looked almost ghostly.

I couldn't say a word for a few minutes. I didn't even move from the elevator, I just stood there in a trance, as I stared at a ghost from my very recent past. It seemed almost like a mirage of sorts, maybe God was playing a trick on me as I looked into the eyes of the woman who had just given me the best sex of my life the night before.

Philly, the sexy seductress from the hotel was staring back at me, her face was telling the same story that my dick was writing inside my draws. As she walked onto the elevator, I quickly faced her direction, unsure of what to do next. Oh shit.

What was she doing here?

Neither of us made any sudden moves as we looked each other up and down. You remember being in school and having to stand near your all time biggest crush. She looked so damn scrumptious though as she stood there before me again. Instant flashbacks rang into my mind as she tried not to look at me. We played that game with our eyes where one of us would look at each other and then look away. I guess it would be up to me to break the ice and start up the conversation.

"What's up Philly? It's nice to see you again." Philly fought smiling as she gave me a dismissive nod and remained looking at her feet.

"Is that all that I get? I mean after what happened at the hot..."

She cut me off and placed a finger near my lips. "HEY. No. Don't do that. Don't bring that up. That was a ONE time thing. You're not supposed to be seeing me right now. I wrote that letter for a reason. What the hell are you even doing here?"

"I work here Philly. If you would've let me tell you more about myself last night you would've known that."

"Work here? You mean work here with me? Are you serious right now?"

"I mean it isn't April. I'm not saying it for a gag little lady. I work on the fifth floor as an editor."

She crossed her arms in a moment of anger, "Wow. This is just great. Very fucking great."

"What's your issue shorty? I thought you'd be cool with it. It's not like I knew you worked here."

"Well, now you do. So do me a favor and act like you don't know me."

"And why is that?"

"Because I don't sleep where I eat. You know how people would react if they knew that we got busy in some hotel one night stand. They would think that I was a hoe. So please just act like you don't know me. Deal?"

Philly got off of the elevator, leaving me salty as hell. So much for continuing with our romance.

Chapter Fourteen

Khali

Meeting with Jo seemed like such a chore for me to accomplish. I hated the idea of having to speak with her at all after what happened to us the last time we had seen each other. I wasn't sure what she could've wanted from me anyway because I had kicked her to the curb so coldly that I thought I was buzzard food. I waited around the restaurant for her arrival, not surprised by her tardiness.

Parker was still in my mind anyway, so she was what I was concerned with as I waited around for my whacky ex to come around. I was literally twiddling my thumbs and sipping on a cup of Sprite waiting for her. Finally, I saw her arrive in her sophisticated arrogance. You couldn't tell Jolani shit about herself. She was the type of woman who thought that it was all about her, and nothing mattered more than herself. She was so cocky that she believed that Prince was singing about her in *Raspberry Beret*. She was one of those arrogant, delusional types.

Jolani walked into the restaurant with her black leather jacket, ignoring the fact that it was hotter than the devil's ball sack outside and sat across from me as she removed her stunner shades. Who the fuck did she think she was? Beyoncé?

"Nice to see that you finally made it Jo," I said sarcastically with a smug look.

"I'm sorry. I had to take care of a few things," she responded back with her lying ass.

"Well, I'm glad that arriving on time wasn't one of those things."

"I'm here ain't I? Don't stress me Khali, I'm not in the mood, and that's not why I wanted you to meet me here."

I slammed my hands on the table and became a little rowdy with her as I asked, "Then what is the point of me being here then Jo? I have things to do."

"Why can't we be civil?"

"Because being civil went out of the window. Our relationship didn't end on the best of terms and you know that."

"And that's why I wanted you to come here Khali. I was wrong. I know I was wrong. I should've been more respectful to your views. I admit that." She tried to grab my hands to which I pulled away from her.

"Now you're saying this? Jolani it's been what a week now? Come on now. What do you really need? Money?"

"No, I don't need money Khali. Why would I need money? I have enough of it. I just want you back."

"Well, I'm not rocking with you on that level anymore."

"And why is that?" she asked with her face smug as a spoiled billionaire.

"Because you're a spoiled, self-entitled prude who only thinks of herself."

"But I can change," she urged with a sense of desperation.

"That's what they all say Jolani. You've even said that before yourself. Actions speak a whole lot louder than words and when it comes to actions, you're as silent as a mouse."

Jolani then stopped arguing with me for a second to simply look at me. She made sure to make consistent eye contact. It was as if she were trying to stare into the depths of my soul.

"Khali what's up with you?"

"What are you talking about Jo? I'm good."

"No you're not. You're trying to get rid of me, and I want to know why. Is there a new hoe in your life? Huh?"

"Jolani what are you talking about?" I said trying to play off her initial question.

"You know what I'm talking about, be real. Who is she?"

"Why does there have to be another girl involved for me to not want anything to do with you?"

"I know you Khali. Now I know that our relationship didn't end the best, but I do know that you wouldn't be pushing me away so quickly. Some little tramp has caught your eye and now you're acting like you're too good to work things out with me. So who is she?"

"Jo, I'm going to be real as can be with you right now. I just don't want anything else to do with you. Our relationship no longer has that kinetic energy to it that it once did. The fire burned out a long time ago. Let's just drop it and move on with our lives got it?"

Jolani in a huff stood up and walked over to me with her finger in my face, "Look here. I love you. You know that I do. You can try to deny the way that you feel about me, but I know you love me too. So, with that being said, if I find out that there's another woman trying to sneak her way to you, I'm going to fuck you both up. I'll be watching you Khali. I'm not the one that you want to piss off."

"And what does that mean exactly Jolani?"

"It means that I'm going to be watching you Khali. Don't have me out here looking stupid. Or I'll have to return the favor to you."

Jolani turned away from me and stormed out of the restaurant leaving me there just thinking *welp that went well.* I knew Jolani well enough to know that she wasn't bluffing. She was a very passionate Aries woman with a constant hunger for attention. I still wasn't worried about her though, she should've been a good woman to me when she had the chance to be.

I was invested in Parker. I wanted to know more about her and her ways now. I was captivated by her from the moment that I met her. Jolani was going to be nothing more than another issue that I didn't need in my life going forward so I wasn't stunting anything that she had to say to me. As I got up to leave, I looked down to see that my little sister Kindness was calling me.

"What's up little Queen?"

Kindness on the other end sounded scared, "Khali hey, I need to talk to you about something."

"What's up little sister?"

"Kojo got kicked out of the house again. He was mouthing off to mom."

I almost broke my phone once she said that. That dude could not seem to keep his head in the game, even after the talk that I had with him earlier.

"And she kicked him out? Where is he at now?"

"He's with Lyric. You know that little trouble making girl from East L.A. Ever since he's been talking to her, he's been getting into all types of stuff. I think he's been hanging around some Bloods too. You have to something Khali. Please. I'm afraid for him, I mean I don't like the way that he talks to mom, but he still needs your guidance more than ever. I don't want to see him hurt on the streets, especially messing with those gang bangers."

I took a deep sigh and said back, "Don't worry, I'll talk to him Kindness. You just keep your head in the books. Your future is what's important. I'll talk to him."

"Thank you, brother. I'll see you soon."

"Coney Island."

"Yes, Coney Island. I can't wait. I love you big brother."

"I love you too Kindness."

I hung up the phone and clamped my hands together to say a quick prayer for my little knuckle head brother. Kojo knew that no matter what he did, he was never supposed to mouth off to Momma Claire. That was a federal offense as far as I was concerned. Our mother did so much for us as kids I don't know where he got off trying to be bigger than her in her own home.

I was going to talk to him alright. I was going to give him the talking to that he needed to have before he really got out of hands. I understood that he was now at the age where he was starting to feel as though nobody could tell him shit. Yeah we'd see about that, I was going to set him straight the way that I told him I would the last time that I got in his face. I hated having to be the bad guy, but somebody had to do it when he wouldn't listen to anybody. If my father was alive, he'd be throwing the hammer down too, so I felt that what I was going to do was going to be in his honor.

California could have it out for you if you let it, so I had to save my brother before things escalated beyond belief and he would have no chance of recovering. All I knew was that, I wasn't about to keep having all of these demons dancing around my aura like this. Shit was about to change in my life, it was bad enough dealing with a crazy ass ex, I wasn't about to let Kojo become a part of the problem too.

Chapter Fifteen

Parker

I had been in the house painting all day. My hands were running across my canvas like they were on crack. I had a full pot of Hazelnut coffee burning, and Maxwell's *Embrya* album made love to my sacred ear drums.

Whenever my mind was locked on something, all I could think to do was paint until my hands bled. I'd be a damn fool to say that Khali wasn't on my mind since we met at the club. Sometimes as women we try not to admit when a guy has done something to our soul, well Khali surely did that. The sad thing was that I didn't give him my number. I had been beating myself about that because it wasn't like me to usually give away opportunities with a guy that fit me.

I just didn't want Khali seeing me as easy, even if I wanted to lick some edible paint off of his chest. Half of me wanted to say fuck it, let's rush and do something dumb. The other half of me said to leave it all up to God, if I was supposed to see him again, I'd see him again. Nothing would stop that. In the meantime, I had bigger fish to fry because my ass was finally getting another chance to exhibit more of my artwork to the *Panache* gallery in two days. They called me early in the morning to initiate the offer to me. It wasn't big like the L.A. Arts Museum that I was determined to get myself into, but it was a start.

So here I was on my carpet painting my newest piece, *The Sisters of Solitude, Struggles and Survival* which was a collage of different historical African American women who had made a difference in my life. I was almost done with it, it was an easy piece to paint, all I had to do was finish the black allure for Michelle Obama's skirt.

"Ooh watch out now chile. You rockin this." I said to myself full of glee.

I was confident that they would like this one, they said that my last one was controversial, but there was no way they wouldn't like this one. Black women were a huge part of your history and I was sure they would love it the way that I did.

If anybody was going to be my number one fan with my work, it was going to be me. Philly would show support every now and then, but she wasn't too big on Art. Unless she was creating a masterpiece inside of her bed with some guy, she was a modern-day Picasso then. I finished up the rest of my painting before I heard my phone begin to ring. Speaking of the sultry devil, it was Philly on the phone, probably with a crazy story of sorts.

"What's up sis?" I asked as I picked up my phone while pouring another cup of coffee, damn near burning myself.

"Girl," she said simply with an exclamation point. When she would start it off with the words *"Girl"* or *"Bitch"* I knew it was something big.

"Aw hell, what done happened chile?"

"GIRL! Tell me why that guy that I banged last night works with me now."

"Wait what?" I said moving my ear closer to the phone to catch all of the tea.

"Yes. You remember the text I sent you this morning about what happened last night? Yes, that dude. Avant. He works at Essence with me. I gave him some fire pussy and now he's trying to work with me."

"Does he work on the same floor as you?"

"No, he works on the fifth floor. He's an editor. Like really?"

"Come on girl, you know you were happy to see him again." I said taking joy out of making her suffer.

"Um, no. I don't sleep where I eat. I mean don't get me wrong, he was good in bed. Well he was better than good actually. I'll give him his props, he was literally the best that I've ever had but that doesn't mean I want to work with him."

"Maybe it's fate girl."

"No, fate is when you get a few hundred dollars more on your taxes than you were supposed to. Fate is when McDonald's fucks up your order and had to give you free food. This is not fate. This is a nightmare waiting to happen. Nothing good can come from this."

"Well look at the bright side, he works on a floor higher than you. You barely have to see him. You don't even have to work alongside him that much. Just keep doing you girl."

"That's the thing. When I saw him in that elevator, I wanted to lick him from his balls to his neck. I was so ready to start up a round two with him, that's why this is such a bad occurrence. I can only avoid him for so long before I flip my lid and jump on his dick like a pogo stick again. I have to avoid him. He looked so damn delicious in that elevator. As delicious as a double chocolate brownie."

I tried to hold my laughter. "Well whatever you do, just be careful, and give it a lot of thought. It'll be alright girl, I'm sure of it. Take a deep breath, let it out, and calm down."

Philly exhaled and continued, "Yeah you're right. You're right and I know it. Anyway, what happened to that guy you were conversing with that night? Did your night end the way mines did?"

I wish that I could say that it did. Philly always sounded so excited to know whether I had lost my virginity or not. I wasn't even going to do my homegirl like that and tell her that Khali took me home, took my virginity, and my soul right along with it. Hell, I wasn't even going to give her the idea that I was even feeling him.

"Girl, I'm not worried about him." I said quickly even though I was lying my ass off because I honestly couldn't stop thinking about him. She wasn't saying anything, but I could feel the disappointment in her voice.

I quickly changed the subject, "That wasn't nothing major. But I can say that I got the call from Panache. They're letting me showcase one of my paintings."

"WHAT?! Look at God. See girl, I told you it would all work out. They finally called back. That's great."

"Yeah, I'm just kind of nervous. I mean this is really my first time showcasing artwork. What if…"

Philly cut me off and started to berate me. "Girl you better not start doubting yourself. Don't make me come over there and slap the shit out of you. You are an amazing talent and I don't ever want you thinking that you're not. One day your art work is going to end up inside of a big ass museum with a casing to keep people from touching it like in the movies. You're going to be big. Don't let those pickle head bougie hoes tell you that your work isn't good enough either."

Now that surprised me, Philly being so overly supportive. I mean she always showed loved but that was literally the sweetest thing that she had ever said to me. I guess I had to eat my words.

"Damn girl. Thank you. That means a lot to me. More than you know."

"Girl no problem, but look, you keep your head up and I'll talk to you later on. Ciao."

"Bye girl, don't get yourself into trouble now."

"I'll try not to. Bye."

I thought closely to what Philly said on the phone and she was right. I couldn't lose faith in myself I had a dream to catch. Of course, it was never easy trying to display African American history at a time when everything we do is considered taboo.

I was going to rock that showcase, as if my life depended on it. Not only that, but I was going to make it my effort to track down Mr. Khali at some point and grab him too. What was the hurt in giving him a try? I pulled up his YouTube channel that he told me about and sat down to listen to some of his poetry. The first poem that came up was entitled *Love Makin.*

Let's make love

Let's make love between the sheets of your warm and cozy bed until our body's surrender.

Let's make the type of love that turns our brains into mesh, the type of love that our minds, our walls, and our neighbors' ears will always remember.

We can get down.

Let's make love in the morning as the sun rays kiss the sides of our faces.

Let's make love to the point where it seems our souls have traded places.

Let's make love in the rain, as God's tears drop onto our naked skin and we melt into each other's arms.

Let's make love during the harshest of winters, the hottest of summers and the most relaxed of falls.

Let's make love inside of a movie theater,

inside of our car.

maybe even a mall.

Let's make love until our neighbors give the cops a call.

We can get down.

Let's make an intense type of love, the type of love that's almost violent in nature as you take out our frustrations on our innocent beings.

You scream in an orgasmic agony that you love me and your hair becomes entangled in my hands.

Let's make a troublemaking type of love,
inside our Bentley Coup until the lights from a
squad car pull up behind us.

Let's make love in silence, no screams, no
fuss.

We can get down.

DAMN.

DAMN.

DOUBLE DAMN.

I had to take a breather after that. Has someone ever been able to bring out the same type of ecstasy that you could get from physicality? Khali's words were that powerful and alluring. I felt as if he were speaking directly to me.

His words were an aphrodisiac for my mind, body, and soul. I was enthralled by his deep voice that sang a song that uplifted my spirits. I practically fell in love with his poetry as I scrolled down to listen more of his work. For the rest of the day, I sat up listening to his work, trying my hardest to not slide in his DM's. I wanted to so badly, because poetry could make my legs shake with an Earthquake's tenacity.

Why didn't I give that man my number?

Why did I always have to be so distant from my suitors?

Why did I feel like this man was my soulmate?

Chapter Sixteen

Philly

I could not believe that Avant had the nerve to work in the exact building as me. What in the hell was God doing to me? Like it wasn't even a full twenty-four hours since I was sucking the color off of his dick. To think that I had to work alongside him every day, every hour, and every second was going to be the worst type of torture. How was I going to be able to look into the eyes of someone who consistently made me think back to our night of tantric sex. Let me clarify that I didn't have a disdain or disregard for him, I didn't want the urge of ripping his clothes off again to come about.

I sat in my office trying to write my newest article, but all I could do was retrace my meeting with Avant. My hands were shaking with how badly I was thinking about this brother. I even began to look at other places of employment because something told me that working with him was going to be trouble. But then again, Parker was right. I mean shit, I really didn't have to bother with him like that if he were on a whole other floor. It wasn't like he was a boiled attached to my ass, the only time he might actually see me was on the elevator.

I just had to calm down was all and keep my composure around him. The only way that I could really cool my jets around him was by being as cold to him as possible, unless there was some type of sign that I wasn't supposed to be cold towards him. The rest of the night, I sat in my office typing away on my newest article as best that I could. I got as far as;

FELLAS,

Read this carefully. A woman's climax is what's truly supposed to matter. If she isn't getting hers off, what's the point of entering the bedroom with her? Are you in the business of simply wasting her time? Are you nothing more than a rabbit humping two-minute magician? One minute you're in and then the next, poof you're gone? Lying next to her sleeping like an infant after a bottle while she stares at you wondering what street corner that she's about to drop you off on? Trust me, we're going to get ours anyway, take your time with her body, treat her body like the temple that it is and remember that she's giving you this chance, you can't disappoint. Could you imagine being hungry beyond belief, waiting all day for a pizza only for the delivery guy to get there with nothing but a box full of crust? Yeah, that's how women feel when we leave them unsatisfied. Pissed off. Looking elsewhere for a full pizza with a two liter Pepsi on the side. We want to be pleasured, we want to be pleased, get it together.

   --Philly

I closed my laptop and saved my work because my brain was being my biggest enemy. I had to get the hell out of there. I didn't have the time, energy or patience to spend another hour at the office. I figured I could do the rest of my work from home. I grabbed my shit and tapped Janae on the shoulder as she spoke on the phone.

   "Girl, I'm out of here for tonight. Hit me up later and we can link. I can't take any more of this day."

   I wanted to avoid possibly seeing Avant again, so I skipped into the elevator trying to hide my face, rapidly pressing the down button as if someone were chasing after me. This was one of those, it was so bad, it was funny type of days. I could damn near taste the wine I was going to open up hitting my lips already. I felt the elevator come to a quick halt, my heart got to beating instantly with fears that it was him coming on.

It wasn't him, but it was that strange dude Javari from earlier. Why are all of the fifth-floor guys so odd? Javari stood close enough to collect body heat from me as I bathed in the smell of his obnoxious cologne. I was just begging for someone to please shoot me in the head, preferably the temple to end this suffering.

"I guess we meet again." He said as he nudged me, almost catching the back of my elbow because of it.

"I guess so?" I said as I rolled my eyes.

Unlike earlier, Javari wasn't as attractive. I don't know whether it was the fact that his breath was smelling like a hot pile of dog shit, or if he just seemed to have this creepy glare in his eyes but I was over it. It seemed that every time I would step away from him, he'd move a bit closer to me too. Like damn nigga give me my space, all of this room in this elevator and you're all on my ass.

"You know Philly. I know this seems kind of out of nowhere, but I'd really like to take you out. Maybe for dinner and a movie."

"In all due respect Javari, I really don't have time to go on a date. I'm kind of distracted right now. Maybe in the future if that's okay with you."

He seemed turned off by my shut down I could see it all in his face. I could've been meaner about it, hell I was really sparing his feelings. I'm sure he probably had some good qualities to him, but I had enough on my plate. I wanted him in the meantime to grab some gum and let his tongue take a piece of it on a date because his shit was bad. I'm guessing he had the raunchy ass supreme taco from catering. The one with the three-day old refried beans. Ugh. See men have to understand that type of shit is detrimental to our image of you. If you're musty, your feet stink, your breath stinks, balls stink, you'll likely never taste me ever. I was going to be calling him *supreme taco* going forward. I'm petty, I know.

I got off of the elevator just in time to not die of suffocation from holding my breath and headed through the doors in a rush. It didn't hit me that I had forgotten my cell phone charger until I had gotten to my car, which fucked me up because it was my only one. DAMMIT. I always seemed to forget something. I was going to need my phone, so I walked swiftly back to the doors. I was walking so fast that I ran right into Avant as he was coming out with a cup of coffee in his hands. A very HOT cup of coffee I might add.

The coffee splashed onto his nice white shirt and spilled onto the middle of my top but luckily, I was wearing black. We both jumped almost out of our shoes at the temperature of the beverage as we both frantically tried to wipe ourselves down. I felt bad because his suit really did look very nice and of course it was my ignorance to my surroundings that caused the accident.

"Oh my gosh, fuck my life! I'm so sorry." I pleaded as he wiped down his shirt.

"No, it's fine really. I was just saying how a coffee stain would make this shirt pop even more than it did." He said back sarcastically as he wiped away at his shirt.

"Don't be a douche. Here, let me help you, it's my fault anyway." I moved his hands away and grabbed a napkin from my purse.

"Philly it's really okay. You don't have to do that."

"Yes I do." I said with a reassuring tone of voice.

"No you don't."

"It's my fault. This whole day has been the wet shits. And what are you even doing here?" I said this as I bent down to wipe the coffee away from the seam of his pants. I stared at the bulge in his crotch area for a moment, tempting myself with a whipping it out and sucking it in broad daylight. *Nope bad Philly. Bad Philly.*

"I thought we already went through this earlier?" Avant exclaimed, snapping me out of my dickmatized trance. Those flashbacks can be something serious man.

"Well I'm still in shock about it so excuse me. I'm not supposed to be seeing you here. We were supposed to fuck each other's brains out and then never see each other again. Now here you are drenched in coffee, still looking good. I don't know whether to add cream to your shirt or rip it off so that I can attack you."

Avant just stared at me with his sexy eyes as I continued ranting, "Well say something."

"I really don't know what to say. I mean what can I say?"

"You can say yes."

"Yes? Yes to what?"

"Yes to me washing your shirt for you. I have some detergent that will get that stain right out in five minutes or less."

"It's cool you don't have to do that."

"But I want to. I'm being nice here Avant, let me be nice."

"Alright, Mrs. Nice. I will let you wash my shirt for me."

"Good. Follow me to my house."

With a look of reluctance, Avant asked back, "Are you sure about this Philly?"

"Yes, I'm sure now get your ass to your car, get in, and follow behind me."

I walked back to my car, completely forgetting the fact that I had to grab my charger from my office. I got in, looked into the rearview, and waited for him to pull up behind me before taking off towards the direction of my house. Now I know what you're thinking. *Philly you said you were going to avoid him at all cost you lying heffa.* Well, look I'm just trying to help and be a good soul. Besides I don't want him walking around with a big ass stain that I caused. I'll fix him up.

Chapter Seventeen

Avant

30 minutes later

I pulled up behind Philly in front of her dope looking condo, to which she signaled for me to pull into her driveway instead of parking on the street. I got out of the car as did she, taking one large look at the exterior of the home. She was living lavishly, the house was in a nice neighborhood, and well gated. Philly even had a garden set up in her backyard.

"This is a nice little place you have here." I said as I followed behind her while she walked to the front door.

"Well thank you sir, I pride myself on having good taste," she said back, giving me flirtatious eyes as he unlocked her door.

"Oh is that right?"

"Yep. I had you didn't I?"

She then opened her front door and allowed me in first. I must say this woman had tons of taste. On each wall of her living room were framed pictures of artist like Prince, Michael Jackson, The Fugees, and Tupac Shakur. She even had a signed guitar from Eric Clapton hanging above one of her leather couches. This woman had it made.

"Damn woman, who did you rob for all of this shit?" I asked jokingly as I removed my blazer.

Philly was in the middle of removing her shoes to show off her pretty feet when she said, "Now see why is it that when a black person has expensive taste, they're accused of being a drug dealer or some shit?"

"Chill woman. It was a joke. I didn't mean to ruffle those pretty little feathers of yours."

"Well ha ha, very funny. You can make yourself comfortable keep your shoes at the door and take off your shirt so that I can place it in the washer. Would you like something to drink?"

I began to strip my upper body as I replied, "I don't know. It depends on what something to drink means." I continued looking around her house, and I came to the realization that this woman was a freak. She had all types of erotic art work hanging up.

She commented back as I observed one of her paintings, "Um well, I have wine, water, milk, and coffee because I know it's your favorite."

"I think I've had enough coffee for one day. I can use a glass of wine though."

"Good because I need a glass too. Is Pinot fine with you?"

"It's great with me."

As Philly squandered around her kitchen, I sat down on her couch to settle down a bit. I wanted to sit still but a part of me also wanted to see what other surprises Philly had waiting for me in her house. They say that you can tell a lot about somebody based on what you see in her home. Well, so far I knew that Philly loved music and sex which was obvious based on our past.

"So, I see you have a lot of paintings in here. A lot of very, detailed paintings."

Philly walked into living room with two glasses of wine in her hands as she nodded to my previous statement.

"Yes well, a lot of those were done by my best friend Parker for my birthday. She's an artist.

I'm not really into art but I support her when I can, and she spent so much time on them that I said what the hell I'll hang them up."

"Well isn't that nice of you. You know that's a strange coincidence my main homeboy Khali does art too. So, I'm sure they'd hit it off."

"I'm sure they would. I guess we have a lot in common." She said as she handed me my glass and stared me down. The tension was so thick, it was crazy. I could feel it, so I knew that she could feel it too. We sat and sipped the wine for a while in silence as our eyes danced around.

Finally, to break the insurmountable tension, I started up another conversation, "So how long have you been working for Essence?"

"Going on four years. Four of the longest damn years of my life. But I would be lying if I said that I wasn't digging every minute of it. I've done every job they've asked of me, I've typed every article, kissed every celebrities ass, and I've indulged in fifteen hundred bottles of wine since working there."

"Impressive. I mean obviously they've treated you accordingly seeing as your living good."

"Look, this all comes from years of taking care of myself and knowing how to spend my money. Plus, I'm a woman who loves being able to treat myself for all of my hard work. Besides, I'll have you know that in a year or so, I don't even plan on working there."

"Really? And what will be your next move?"

"I don't know. I've always had this dream of starting my own magazine or maybe taking a year off to write my first memoir. Since last year, I've wanted to start my own memoir for a while, maybe some type of erotica novel, I don't know. But I do see myself being on the beaches of Peru or Costa Rica as I write. Momma needs a tan."

She watched me sip my wine for a second as she stopped talking. It was like she got off on watching me enjoy it. Philly had this way of looking at you that could bring a weaker man to his knees, begging her for mercy. If I could sit and look into the fireplace in her eyes all night I would.

"So enough about me. Tell me more about you Mr. Avant."

"What do you want to know Mrs. Philly?"

"Hmm, let's see. Maybe like where you're from. Have you ever been married or better yet, what possessed your fine ass to come to my place of business and make it your own?"

After a sly and uncomfortable laugh, I placed my cup of wine down as she awaited an answer from me.

"Okay, well I'm from Georgia. Atlanta to be exact, born and raised. I've never been married, not even close to being married. And as far as your last question, I was hired by Cheryl before I even moved here. I had sent feelers from Atlanta and after a few phone calls, I was given the job if I could relocate. Which I did. I needed a change of location anyway."

"And why was the need for a change of location so necessary?"

"Let's just say that there was a lot about Georgia that I wanted to leave behind for good."

Philly whisked her glass of Pinot before asking, "So you decided to come here, snatch my soul and then work next to me so that I could suffer in silence every day?"

"It wasn't my intention on, as you say, make you suffer in silence. I was taking an opportunity for success. You just happened to come along and give me the best welcome to L.A. gift that a man could ever ask for. So thank you for that."

The blushing Philly gave me a smile and asked, "You just think you're so damn charming don't you?"

"Obviously you think so. Otherwise what happened between us wouldn't have happened."

"Okay, let's set some things straight my dude. I love sex, okay? I love sex and sex loves me. I've never been with a guy longer than three months and usually those three months consist of hot, fiery, love making in any venue available. After that, I drop guys like flies because they no longer interest me. I'm a thirty-year-old single sex addict with a head full of greed and a bulletproof heart. I do think that you're an attractive male. But don't assume that what happened with us, you know the whole dance off with our pants off, was anything but a wild one-night stand. Guys like you don't last too long with me."

"And why is that?"

"Because you bet cocky. You start to believe that because I let you taste me that you have me under your spell well you're wrong. And when you're wrong, it's easy for me to break your ass down and make you shine my crown."

Philly's face was no longer one that was full of smiles, she was now dead ass serious with a determined stare. Philly got up from her seat and walked back to her laundry room leaving me there to awkwardly stare at her walls. This entire situation felt weird. I mean, here I am sitting in the house of a woman that I had a drunken one-night stand with, shirtless, with a strange boner growing in my pants. This wasn't exactly the way I envisioned ending my night, but it could be worst. I could hear Philly rumbling around before she walked back in.

"Your shirt is in the dryer," she said as she sat back down.

"Look, I didn't mean to offend you Philly. I just thought that we had a bit of chemistry."

"And we do. But that doesn't mean that it's the type of chemistry that I would like to study more. Besides, I was pretty bad at chemistry back in high school. You feel me?"

"Yeah I feel you. Well, can I at least get a tour of the rest of the house?"

Philly contemplated it before giving in to my request, "I guess I can do that for you. Since I like being nice."

With a slight look of reluctance, she grabbed my hand to help me stand up before leading me out of the living room. I couldn't help but look at her ass it swayed back and forth. I wanted to wrap my hands around her hips so badly. I had so many women in my time, but there was something about Philly that made my body turn hot as a furnace. She was the type of woman who was a danger to the mind, an addiction to the body and a substance for the heart. In other words, Philly was the greatest drug known to mankind.

Philly first led me into her personal library hooked up with enough erotica to start her own damn Barnes and Nobles. She hooked the area up. I mean she had so many big-time names on her shelves, Zane, Eric Jerome Dickey, Carl Weber, she was packing with novelists.

"Welcome to my personal getaway. When I step in here with a glass of Moscato or Pinot, I pick up one of these books and go into another universe."

"Yeah, I see that. Oh shit. I also see that you have the Sex Chronicles here!" I said hyped up, grabbing it off of the shelf.

"What you know about the Sex Chronicles?" she asked as she sat down on one of the chairs inside the library.

I laughed, scrolled through the pages, and then said, "I know a whole damn lot. If anybody would know that, it would be you."

"Yeah, whatever. I'll admit you put it down on me. But there's a lot about the Sex Chronicles that stole my life aside from just the sex scenes. Please believe me, the sex was great, but her imagery was off the charts. There's just something about a good Zane book that can make your toes curl and have you sweating up a storm in your sheets."

"I'm guessing you've read it more than once."

"More than once, baby boy I've read it enough times to memorize the entire book without looking at it. The scenes seem so real, so tantric. I have a thing for anything…tantric."

Philly had her eyes locked squarely on my dick as she sipped the last remnants of her wine. I closed my eyes for a second, picturing her being bent over one of those as I fucked her like one of the characters from the *Sex Chronicles*. With a ball of her hair entangled in between my fingers as I pulled back on it, fucking her from the back. I could hear her moaning my name, almost singing it in my ear as I grinded inside of her. My dick was doing backflips inside of my pants.

"You ready to see the rest of the house?" she asked quizzically as she stood back up. My mind flashed back to reality the moment I heard her voice.

"Um, yeah, yeah let's go."

"Okay, follow me," she said as waved me on with her pointer finger.

We then next headed upstairs, her hallway walls were covered in more portraits and pictures of her posing with other celebrities. She then led me to a room with her door closed, standing in front of it to block me from walking in right away.

"What's the matter?" I asked as she placed a hand on the door knob of the room.

"This is my bedroom. I usually don't let men into my master bedroom right away. Most men stay downstairs by my fireplace, or I take them into my guest room. It's always been somewhat of a privacy thing with me."

"A privacy thing?"

"Yeah, you know how some women won't allow a man to kiss them until a certain time, or maybe won't allow them to meet their parents? Well, I don't bring too many men into the place I sleep. Until I get a good enough vibe from them.

So with that being said, welcome to my Master bedroom."

Philly opened the door and allowed me inside of her bedroom. My eyes instantly diverted to the bed, covered in black satin sheets, big enough to fit an entire family. Thoughts ran into my mind of her being sprawled over that said bed, with my body on tops of hers. I could feel the warmth of from her pussy as my face drew near it, and my tongue did a slow dance over her clit.

I looked over to my right and could see that she still had old records and CD's as collector items.

"Dayum. You've got quite a stack here woman. Oh shit, is this Joe." I said picking up her old Joe's greatest hits albums.

"Yeah, you know I had to have Joe. You can claim to be a love making specialist if you don't have Joe in your house, come on now. He's like the king of love making tracks. It's funny, I have all of these CD's and I don't even own a CD player anymore. I sold the last one that I had. Everything is stored on my phone now with today's technology you know?"

"Yeah I know. That doesn't mean we still can't get down a bit."

"What?" she said with a curious smile on her face.

I grabbed my phone and went to Joe's *Let's Stay Home Tonight* on my Spotify account to allow it to play. I tried to dance, the keyword to that is try because I know that I couldn't dance worth shit. Philly was trying to hold back her giggles as I strutted towards her trying to be as smooth as possible.

With her hands on her head, laughing uncontrollably she said to me, "Oh my Lord Avant. You dance like you have two left feet and they both left from under you."

"Dance with me." I urged grabbing her soft hand and pulling her to me.

"You are crazy."

"Crazy? Yes. But I still want to dance."

Philly started to rock her hips side to side a bit before backing up on me. She grinded across my waist the same way that she did when we met at the club, this time with more passion because we were in private.

"You better be lucky that I love to dance mister."

"Show me don't tell me." I challenged of her as I spun her sexy ass around to get a close look at her face, her lips, and her eyes.

"You remember this? Me holding you like this at the club?"

"Yes, and I also remember getting you hard as a rock when I got close to you. Just like how I am now. Your breathing became heavy, you couldn't control your body's tempo. You fell in love with me on that dance floor didn't you?"

"Maybe I did. Maybe, you were too intoxicating to pass up on."

Philly grabbed my phone and said, "How about we switch the song to something slower."

She grabbed the phone and glowed at the sight of something that she saw, "Ooh, I see you've got this on here."

Maxwell's *A Woman's Worth* started playing and she got close to me again. She wrapped her arms around me and placed her lips near my ear. My hands began to maneuver down to her waist, firmly placed, as we slowly danced in her room. The feel of her soft breasts pushing up against my chest exhilarated my blood stream. I could feel her nipples beginning to excitedly harden.

As the melody of the song began to make love to my ears, I got the urging to make love to her body. I wanted her pussy across my face again. I wanted to feel the vibration coming from her shaking legs as she was riding me. I began to squeeze her ass as we danced slowly, her body would seem to pulsate as I would squeeze tighter.

"You better stop," she said flirtatiously in my ear.

"Or what?"

"Or you'll get something started."

"Oh really?"

"You know I don't lie."

I wanted to challenge her to see what she would do if I decided to take things further. I continued to squeeze both of her ass cheeks in the palms of my hands. She bit her lip, and then bit the bottom of my ear lobe to get me going. I felt the tip of her tongue go down the side of my neck, making my blood rise, making my heart began to beat tremendously.

Neither of us was supposed to be doing this and we knew it, but she smelled so good in my arms, she was contagious.

With my lips now attacking the corner of her neck, in specific the corner behind her ear, I whispered, "Come and get this dick. It's yours."

Philly looked up at me, shocked, but ready to take what I was offering to her. She nodded and grabbed a handful of it while I wrapped a hand around her neck to kiss her passionately. We had already done this song and dance once, so there was no stalling this time. I picked her up into my arms as we began to kiss like our lives were on the line.

"You sure you want this again Big Daddy?" she asked as she violently slapped me, knowing that it turned me on.

"Hell yeah, so shut up and take it."

"Make me," she said back while biting her soft and ready lips.

I grabbed her by the hair to make her do just that, pulling her back to me as we kissed again. My hands were grabbing all over her ass, her legs were wrapped around my waist, and our need for each other was almost to the point of an addiction.

Philly jumped down from my arms and pushed me onto the bed in a sensual rage before straddling me. I watched as she kissed across my pecs, stomach, and my shoulder blades which felt almost euphoric. She then grabbed both of my arms and raised them above my head, contrary to me being in control the last time. Philly loved feeling as if she were the one in control.

I placed one of my hands across her neck as she worked over my upper body with her lips, intensifying the situation by sucking on both sides of her neck. She had this way of kissing you that could put you to sleep if you let her, her lips were like two big ass pillows.

I rolled over and took over where she left off, kissing across her chest. I squeezed both of her titties, and then started to rip off her bra but she placed a finger to my lips. I responded by sucking on that finger, making her want it even more, she sucked on it too before pushing me off her.

"What's wrong with you?" I asked, trying to catch my breath from that wild moment of ecstasy between us.

"Nothing, it's just that, I have to get your shirt from the dryer."

I said back aggressively, "Oh woman fuck that shirt."

"No, I need to get it."

"Are you being dead ass serious with me right now Philly?"

"It'll just be a second."

Philly got up and took off out of the room without another moment. She just left me with my dick high in the air, and the romance dying faster than a Grey's Anatomy patient. I sat on the bed, scrolling on my phone as she took her sweet time getting my phone from the laundry room.

As I was looking at my Facebook page to kill time, I could hear her calling my name from downstairs.

I got up from where I was sitting and headed to the laundry to see where she was. I could hear her voice, but I had to follow to the direction of it to see exactly where she was. I continued to follow her voice until I got to a room on the far end of her first floor. Imagine my excitement when I walked in on her sitting completely naked on top of the washing machine. The machine was still rocking, and her body was looking ready to pounce on.

"Your shirt is dry," she said in a cunning voice with my shirt draped across her neck. She used the shirt to pull me closer to her, picking up where we left off in her bedroom.

I wasted no time in licking all around her titties again, sucking each nipple until she hollered out in an orgasmic fury. She slapped me again, and then wrapped her around legs around my neck as her way to tell me what she wanted next. Well, let me tell you that there was nothing better than a clean, shaved pussy that was calling my name. I cherished every moment of kissing across both of her warm, candy thighs. I became possessed with her reaction to me taking my tongue from her thighs down to the flap of her clit to make her shiver.

She watched as I circled the tip of my tongue around her vulva, curling it across her clit, and then bouncing it repeatedly across each of her lips to make her cry out again in a primal yell. I watched her eyes roll into the back of her head as I rhythmically kissed, licked, and then explored her walls with my wide tongue. I didn't care if she came five times in a row I was going to keep tasting.

"Shhhit." She said as her body vibrated in rhythm to the shaking washing machine that her back was sprawled across.

"This is what you wanted right?" I said antagonizing her seductively.

"Fuck you. I hate you right now. I swear that shit feels so good."

I had a face full of her wet, warm pussy all across my face, giving my chin a chance to shower in her juices. I wanted to own her body. I wanted her to put some respect on my name. This was more than just eating her pussy, through her pleasure I was ultimately receiving mine as well. If I didn't eat that pussy properly the last time, this time I was going to eat it good enough, she would question the niggas she fucked with in the past.

This was the type of pussy eating that would be having me always on her mind; my tongue was determined to make her mine. She grinded across my face, my tongue was deep inside of her woman hood, and she moaned approvingly. Her eyes then grew wide, bewildered in fact as she pulled me down close to her.

"Fuck me," she demanded as she grabbed my neck. "Fuck me now!"

I didn't get a chance to truly react to that because she then unbuckled my belt, as my hand remained across her pussy and massaged her G-Spot. She never took her eyes off of me as she flicked a devious smile and groped my dick with both of her hands.

The moment I dropped my pants, she took my dick deep inside of her for the second time in twenty-four hours. I loved watching her bite her lip as I slid it deep inside of her, her deep gasp enticed my soul, and the feeling of her warm walls clenching around my shaft elevated my adrenaline. She took of all of this dick like nobody before her every could. It was as if she were riding a roller coaster. Her hands were pasted onto the washing machine, her legs wrapped around me and her arms around my neck.

"Take this shit. Yeah just like this." I said empathically into her ear as she kissed m neck in return.

I loved the fact that she was so precise with her touch, her kisses, and her ways of knowing exactly what to do next.

I slid inside and out of her slowly to watch her body fall into a hypnotic trance. I wanted to fuck her all around her house, and as great as the laundry room is, I wanted to explore a bit. I picked her up into my arms to literally walk her around her house with me still inside of her. I slammed her against one of her walls, fucking her up against it, she screamed so loudly that the entire city could hear my name being screamed.

Philly scratched my back, digging deep enough that she could've tattooed it with her sharp nails. Her digging only made my stroke game more intense, lethal almost, and she was loving every second of the pain that I was putting her through. I then walked with her again, bringing her into the living room where I let her down but placed her over the couch.

As she rested over the couch, I entered her again, fucking the life out of her with back shots with my hands across her neck. My dick was covered in her sweet nectar, her cum was giving it the wettest shower that it ever had. I had her arms interlocked with mine, pulling back as I fucked the life out of her. This was the position that separated the men from the boys, and I proved my worth to her as the man she needed to be fucking here.

I finally pulled out of her and got to eating her pussy from the back with a finger in her ass to really make her cum for me.

"Oh shit!" she screamed to the Heavens as she pushed my face in further.

I loved being inside of her, but I loved my tongue being inside of her even more than that. I swirled my tongue around her swollen lips and kissed every spot of it before my tongue explored the rim of her ass too. Her climax hit my face like a warm sprinkler in the summer time. I took all of it and licked it from across my lips like the remaining drops of an ice cream cone. I then left her there across the couch, as she looked back at me in shock like *damn nigga is that how it is?*

"Why? Why did you do that to me with that dick of yours?" she asked in between heavy breaths.

"You asked for it. You wanted that round 2 as badly as I did. Admit it."

"Shit, a round 2? I need a full 12 rounds fucking with you."

"And I'll break your shit down every single round too."

"I'm going to get you back Avant. Don't think it's over."

I turned her around, kissed her again and then said, "I wasn't expecting it to be. How about we make these little sessions we keep having a daily thing? We can have that nobody needs to know type of situation. Deal?" She kissed me back and silently said deal as she continued recuperating from another wild ride with me.

Chapter Eighteen

Philly

The Next "Moan" in

It had been a long time since I had woken up next to a man. I usually kick niggas out of my house after I get mine off, but Avant was something serious I have to admit. We fucked so much the night prior that I felt that staying over was the best solution. The way his ass put me in a slumber not once, but multiple times, was more than enough to have me on his side for good. Avant wanted to continue our sex sessions on a daily basis which I had no issue with, I mean it was just sex right? We both knew what we were getting into, so I didn't have to worry about strings being attached.

I did think that he deserved some breakfast though after fucking me into another decade the way that he did. That didn't make him my man or anything, but I was sure he was hungry after the night we had. I should've made his ass wake up and make me breakfast for almost paralyzing me with his stroke game. I slipped into my closet, slipped on a black silk robe, and headed downstairs while he slept like a baby.

Once I got into my kitchen, I put on some Maxwell's French Roast coffee and pulled out ingredients to make pancakes and eggs. As I started to cook, I decided to call Parker because I had to tell someone about how good this man put it down on me. I did a little dance as the phone rang, and once she picked up, I got as ratchet as I could get.

"Hello?"

"What's up my whore?! Good morning."

After a shy laugh she responded with, "Good morning. You're in a good mood early this morning. I guess you had a good night."

"Girl a good afternoon and a good night. I promise you, I haven't a night like the one I had last night in a LONG time. You remember that guy that I was telling you about?"

"Yeah, the one-night stand guy from the club right?"

"Yes, girl, he put it down something proper last night."

"What? I thought you weren't going to sleep with him again?"

"Well sue me because I lied to ya ass. He came over, and things heated up. Girl he tore my little ass up. I'm in this kitchen making him breakfast and you know I don't cook for anybody."

"Well damn girl, I'm happy for you. So, what does that mean you two are together now? Because you haven't had a boyfriend in I don't know how long."

I almost choked on my coffee as I answered back. "Girl stop. He's not my boyfriend. We just agreed that the sex is too good to not indulge in. I think we can handle having sex and a bit of romance without actually being together."

"Hmm, well you just be careful. Hopefully this one lasts longer than three months."

"Yeah, we'll see babes. We'll see. But look, I have to go. I'll see you tomorrow at your showcase okay?"

"Okay but wait Philly, before you go I have a suggestion. Why don't you bring your little friend with you? I have a few extra tickets to spare, I'm sure he would enjoy it."

"Maybe so. I'll think about it because I don't want him getting the wrong idea. But I'll run it by him. But let me finish making this man's breakfast. I'll see you later babes. Love you."

"Love you too bye-bye."

Parker was right, Avant would love to come to her showcase. I just didn't want him thinking that we were together because of it. Then again, he was fucking me and about to eat something other than my pussy for once so who knows what he was about to think.

I finished making his breakfast of golden brown pancakes, complete with a side of whipped cream and fruit on the side. I added to it a cup of coffee, my special scrambled eggs that were spiced a bit with Cajun seasoning and bacon too. I knew how to hook shit up when I had to. I crept back upstairs without much sound, Avant was still sleeping, but I changed that when I gave him a few kisses across his lips.

"Wake up mister."

Avant's eyes opened slowly to the sight of the breakfast that I prepared for him. They always say that the best way to the man your fucking's heart is food, right? I think that's how it goes; well that's how it goes in my mind.

"Oh damn, well look at this. You did all of this for me, huh?"

"Yup, only because you gave me my meal last night."

"Well, I appreciate this. This looks damn good, if it tastes as good as you did last night, I'm in for a treat."

"Such a smooth talker. Well eat up."

I watched him eat for a minute before growing some balls and asking him the question that was going to make everything weird for me.

"Avant, I have something to ask you. It's kind of important."

"What's up?" he asked with a mouth full of food.

"Remember yesterday when we spoke about my friend Parker's art showcase?"

"Yeah, what about it?"

"Well, she had a few extra tickets and I was wondering if you maybe wanted to come. I mean it's not a date or anything, you can bring a friend if you'd like to. Just throwing out the invitation. That's all."

"I'd love to come."

I stared at him for a second before saying back, "You sure?"

"I'm positive. I'd love to come. I'll bring my homie Khali, and we'll have a good time. Maybe afterwards we can do something together."

I was trying to act like I wasn't as happy as put on to be, but truth be told I was. I was geeked as hell. I didn't even understand why, I mean Avant was supposed to just be another guy to me, but he was doing numbers in my mind. He was making my heart jump more than a sip from a Mojito. I hadn't had so many goosebumps on my arm since I first heard Shalamar perform live.

"Okay, cool, I can't wait. Wear your best suit and if you smell like anything less than the cologne you've been wearing, don't approach me."

"You know you have a lot of suggestions and demands for somebody who was begging to keep hitting that one spot behind your ear last night."

"Hey, look, I like being pleased okay! Now shut up and eat. We have work in two hours."

"Oh shit, we do have work, don't we?" he said in a panic. "Shit, I have to go home and get changed."

"Relax Avant. You have time to eat and then head home to get dressed in one of your little fancy suits. So, sit back down and eat mister goody two shoes."

"Is that another suggestion?"

"Nope, that's a damn demand."

Avant grabbed me by my waist and kissed me with a strawberry in his mouth. Obviously, he was trying to get something started with me, if only he knew how dangerous that was. I was the type to go all day, and all night.

"See there you go again trying to get something started with me."

"Is it working?" he inquired with his intoxicating, massaging tongue running across my shoulder.

"Maybe. But, we'll have to wait until later. If I give you another round now, you won't be able to move which messes with your money and mine too. So eat your food, drink your coffee, and I'm going to get in the shower."

"Whatever you say, little woman."

I rolled my eyes at him and slipped into the shower as he ate. This was a shower that I truly needed after the last few nights with Avant. That man brought this sexual energy with him that resurged my entire body. So when I felt his strong hands wrap around my sopping wet shape in the shower, I took all of the pride in the world in giving him the next round that I promised to not give him initially. This man was driving me crazy.

Chapter Nineteen

Khali

"I'm telling you now Kojo, if I have to have this conversation with you again, I'm going to bust you up worse than I already did. You hear me?" I screamed at my little knuckle head ass brother as I yelled in his face in the alley of my ma's home.

I had just gotten done beating him like he stole something to knock some sense into him. Now I know what you're thinking, I went too far right? But let's be real, the reason that a lot of knuckle heads can get away with the things that they do is lack of a discipline. All of the news reports of car jackings, youths killing each other and adults, I refused to watch my brother end up on the wrong track. If that meant putting paws on him every now and then I'd do that.

"Look at you Kojo, look at you. You have everything! You have a mother and family that cares about you, money, and food. What the hell is wrong with you? Do you see how crazy shit is out here? How people love snatching up little knuckleheads like you and popping you one? You see how some of these cops love putting young, black kings like you out for LESS than what you do? I don't want to see you hurt or worse because you don't want to get your shit together. Look at your sister she's a young, black, educated princess who is on the verge of BIG THINGS. You could be one in the same. You better get yourself together and show ma more respect got it?"

I grabbed him by the collar of his neck and said again, "I said you got it?"

"Yes man, I got it."

"GOOD. Now take your black ass in the house, tell Ma you apologize for your lack of respect, get on your homework because I will be calling your teachers to make sure that it's done and show respect to the Queens of the house. We better not have to have this conversation again man."

Kojo kept his head down and I pulled him back to hug him tightly. I had hoped that my message had gotten through to him because he seemed to be convinced that I wasn't playing around. Of course, it could have all been smoking mirrors though. I watched Kojo go back inside, as Mama Claire watched from the mirror with a proud look on her face. I told her that I would be the man of the house even though I was no longer living there and that's what I meant.

As I walked back down the street, I could see that Avant was calling me. I hadn't heard from my boy since he got all moved in, so I was interested to see how everything was going with him.

"What's up my homie?" I asked enthusiastically as I picked up my phone.

"Man, what's going on Khali,"

"Shit, had to take care of Kojo again."

"Oh yeah, he's giving you problems again, huh?"

"Yeah same situation, petty shit that I had to squash before it got out of hand. You know how that is."

"Yeah, I know how that is man. But listen man, I have something to run pass you and want you to hear me out on this."

"I'm listening what's good?"

"You know I met this little lady at the club you brought me to my first night in L.A. right? So, she gave me an invite to this art showcase tomorrow and I was wondering if you wanted to head up with me? I mean since you're more of an artist than me."

"Art showcase eh? Sounds like my type of party. Where is this art showcase going to be held at?"

"The Panache Gallery. You know that place right?"

"Yeah I do. Tomorrow you say? Hmm. Sounds like a plan. I'll be there man."

"Aight bet. Oh, and she has a friend by the way man. So, keep that in mind. See you tomorrow bro, seven pm. I'll scoop you up."

"Bet. See you then man."

After I hung up, I went back home with motivation to start a small portrait of mine own. Going to an art showcase sounded like fun especially after everything I had been going through lately. I needed some fun in my life. Badly.

Part Four

The Portrait of My Heart

Chapter Twenty

Philly

The Art Showcase

The Panache Gallery was full of a bunch of saddity people who thought that they knew more than you because they knew how to work a paint brush. But it was my homegirl's night, so I promised to behave myself and show her massive love. I was so proud of her. She deserved to have her artwork hanging in someone's gallery, and it was a long time coming.

Parker was visibly shaking, nervous as all hell is more the phrase to use, but she was so damn pretty in her all black dress. She was just standing in one spot, afraid to move as all of these famous artists were mingling amongst themselves. I tapped Parker on the shoulder and said, "Girl get out there and introduce yourself. Your showcase is coming up in thirty minutes, so it'll help you ease the tension."

"I know girl. I know it's just that I'm surrounded by so many well-known artists. How can I expect them to take me seriously? What if they don't like my work?"

"What did I tell you about saying what if? What if Obama decided not to run for President? What if Martin Luther King Jr., the Black Panthers', and Malcolm X decided that they weren't going to take a stand for our people? What if Tupac or Beyoncé never made music? Hell, what if Ruby Bridges decided to get homeschooled and Rosa Parks never sat down in that white man's seat? You see Parker, when God gives you a chance to become Black excellence, you take it. You are a talented Black artist, and a talented BLACK woman who has every right to be here with all of these sticks in the mud. Black art is beautiful. Hell, Black is beautiful art. So, don't make me slap you. Now take a sip of your wine and go over there to mingle with those white people. I'll be watching too."

Parker looked shocked at my aggressive attitude, but I needed her to realize that her success meant everything to me. I believed in her because she always believed in me. I felt bad because in the past, I had not truly believed in her the way that I should've, so this was my chance to really make a change for the better with her. We all needed somebody to be there for us and that was what I was there for. Parker slowly moved over to the other artist as I stood with my glass of Moscato even though it seemed very watered down. I walked around to observe some of the artwork which didn't look too bad, but Parker's work was going to give this place a face lift.

I looked down at my phone because Avant was running late, and Parker was going to be introducing her piece soon. It was looking more and more as if he wasn't going to show up which was pissing me off because I had put faith in him. I had put more faith in him than I had in any other guy in recent memory.

"I knew I shouldn't have invited him." I whispered to myself in self-doubt as I looked at my watch again in anger.

As soon as I put my phone back into my purse, I looked over to see him and his guy walking in. My heart began to ease up and I was relieved that I wasn't going to have to kill him for not showing. Avant saw me watching him from a far distance and walked over to me looking dapper as all Heaven in his black tuxedo. His homie wasn't looking too shabby either in his white blazer.

"Well look what the cat dragged in." I said jokingly as he hugged me.

"That must be a sexy ass cat to have dragged me in here. Philly this is my best friend Khali, blogger, artist, and poet."

I shook hands with Khali and recognized him instantly.

"Oh wait. I do know you. I've seen a lot of your videos you're a big hit there mister. Well nice to meet you formally."

"The pleasure is all mine Philly. Thank you for inviting me. This is definitely my type of event here."

"Well don't thank me, this is my friend Parker's event."

Khali's face dropped, and he said back to me, "Parker? Did you say Parker?"

"Yeah, Parker. She's the star of tonight's event. She's right over there."

A huge grin grew over Khali's face and without another thought he walked over to Parker as she spoke to some of the other guests. I guess he saw something that he liked in her because he walked over with a fire under his ass.

"What was that all about?" I asked to Avant who shrugged back at me in return.

"Well I'm glad that you could make it. I was starting to think that you were going to no show and I would have to kick your ass."

"I thought about it, but I said to myself, I have nothing better to do anyway."

"Ha-ha, very funny asshole."

Avant then became serious as he placed a hand on my hip. "Well. You know that I wouldn't miss it for the world."

"Hmm, you must want the neck or something?"

"Maybe I do. I mean I deserve some type of reward, right?"

"I'll be the judge of that. You just be patient, I have a little surprise waiting for you at my house tonight."

"Oh, is that so?"

"It's very so."

"Well can I have a hint at this surprise?"

I grabbed his dick and then whispered to him seductively, "Do you like grapefruit?"

"I'm not against a citrus product every now and then."

"What about fruit roll ups?" I asked squeezing tighter.

"If these questions are heading to where I think they're heading, you know the answer to them all is a definite yes."

"Good, we'll see how much you can handle tonight then. Until that time, let's give all the attention to my girl Parker. It's her night."

Chapter Twenty-One

Parker

I was so nervous trying to fit in with the rest of the other artists at the gallery. My showcase was in ten minutes and my heart was practically ripping through my chest. I was trying to think of any way to ease the nervousness, but it really wasn't working too well. I was standing next to this one artist in particular, Martin Samuel III who was a know it all. I couldn't even get a word in because he would cut me off every time I tried.

Just by looking at him you knew he was a snob; a caviar and crackers extraordinaire who wasn't familiar with where I came from. He was also pretty insensitive to African American history because all that mattered to him was his own history.

Martin spoke with this very sophisticated accent and would say things like, "You see this painting, this is history right here. American history at its finest."

I decided to speak up and ask confidently, "What about African American history?"

"I beg your pardon?" He rebutted with his snobbish tone of voice.

"I said with all due respect sir, what about African American history? I mean we have a significant place in art history too."

"Well with all due respect to you madam, I don't believe so. Most significant painters are Caucasian American, sorry to inform you. Maybe if this were a rap gallery you'd have a point."

Now see I could've punched him for that but before I could, I heard a voice come from the background.

"That may be true sir. But if I may, allow me to add a few things in response to what my sister said."

I turned around to see Khali walking up to the man, and my heart began to skip a beat. What the hell was he doing here? I was more nervous than ever now, I was expecting him to be here.

Khali continued. "You see sir. You're right. We do have significant history in rap music. I mean we aren't as defined as Beethoven or whatever the fuck you listen to in your five-thousand-dollar mansion with your Donald Trump poster hanging above your wall, but it is nice though. However, I think our place in art is also pretty significant, you see there have been a lot of great Black artists contrary to what you believe. I mean check out my lady to your right, tonight is her showcase. I bet you didn't even know that did you?"

The man tried to speak but Khali cut him off. "Hell no you didn't. But let me give you a little history lesson, James Stidum. You know that name? He was one of the first Black painters in history. Jacob Lawrence is another. You want more? How about Meta Warren Fuller? In 1914 she created the piece known as the Ethiopia Awakening which anticipated a resurgence of sorts in African themes during the Harlem Renaissance. You have to know Alma Woodsey Thomas though don't you? Her paintings were the first to get a solo exhibit inside of Whitney Museum. She was the first African American woman to do so as a matter of fact at the age of 80. One of her pieces actually is sitting on a wall right behind you. You see if you actually knew your art you would've known that. But you just figured all we were good at was rapping and eating chicken, huh?"

Martin tried to eat humble pie as he said, "I humbly apologize sir. I meant no disrespect."

Khali shook his head, placed a hand on Martin's shoulder, and said, "None of your people seem to mean any disrespect until somebody checks you on it. Now I believe that you owe my lady over there an apology for your bullshit and un-philosophical rhetoric on our people."

Martin then approached me and said as he shook my hand, "I'm very sorry madam. I look forward to your showcase."

"You bet your ass you're looking forward to it." Khali added in as he observed the paintings in the background.

Martin walked away as I just stood there staring at Khali like my socially conscious knight in shining armor. I didn't know how he got there but I was glad that he did.

"What the hell are you doing here?" I asked smiling like a little girl standing next to her crush at Valentine's Day party. I honestly couldn't believe that I was staring dead at him again after our night at the club.

"I was invited. I heard that there was a showcase here tonight. I had no idea that it was your showcase though. I'm glad that it is because Parker you have been on my mind all week since we met at the Club. It seems that we always run into each other at the most opportune times huh?"

"I guess so. I can honestly say that I'm glad that you came. It seems that God doesn't want us to be apart."

"Not in the slightest."

We stared at each other until our eyes began to make love to each other. It was obvious that we wanted to know more about each other. I was digging him. Khali was such a sexy piece of milk chocolate. Being in his presence made it easier for me to get comfortable at the showcase. All of the tension was starting to ease, and I was feeling like the Queen of the Throne for one night at least.

Philly and her guy approached me. Philly was giving me that *what's going on here* type of look.

"Parker this is Avant. The guy I've been telling you about. Kind of."

Philly then looked at us and said, "Well I see you two know more about each other than I realized. I've been watching you two for a minute over in the cut."

I responded with, "Yeah this is Khali. We met at Club Joi, he's a poet and a painter."

Philly placed her hands on her hips and said to Khali, "Oh so you're just good at everything huh? Well how about you do my taxes since you're multi-talented."

Khali said back in return, "As long as I can get half."

I playfully slapped him on the shoulder, looked down at my phone, and realized that it was time for the showcase. My legs began to shake, and my body started to get warm. I was getting nervous all over again.

"Shit, it's time guys. Lord Jesus I'm so nervous."

Khali rubbed my shoulders, "Hey. You're going to do great. You hear me? It's going to go amazingly."

"Thanks Khali. Your being here is calming my spirit I must admit."

"And what about me?" Philly asked arrogantly but joking with me nonetheless.

"Girl ain't nobody stuntin' you. Well I'm about to get set up so I'll you guys in a bit."

I walked away from the crew to walk over to my painting that was being covered by a red sheet. The director of the night's event signaled to me that she was ready to start, and I gave her the say so to bring the audience over to me as I stood in front of the painting.

The director, whose name was Marissa Clay, cleared her throat, and began.

"Attention. If I could have all of your attention now, we're about to start tonight's showcase. If I could have you all gather around so that I can formally introduce tonight's talented young artist. She hails from right here in California, and she has a very special piece that comes straight from the heart. Let me introduce you all to Parker Massey."

I took a deep breath, stepped up to the crowd after the applause stopped, and said to the crowd of onlookers, "As a Black woman, a lot of times, I get discouraged from really attempting to find my niche in society. Reason being, that I truly never knew what my true niche was. But as I stand before you today, I would first like to say that I'm elated to have been given this opportunity. Secondly, I would like to introduce my piece to you all through a testimony. When I was a young girl, I was an only child, coming from a hardworking mother who worked three jobs and a father who was barely around. When he was around, he would abuse my mother, he would abuse her, and he would abuse me too, sexually and physically. I went through my teenage years afraid, secluded, and discouraged. Until, a strong Black woman who happens to be my best friend began to rebuild my faith. She means so much to me. So, in honor of her, my mother and strong Black women around the world, I would like to present my piece."

I ripped the red sheet off and said as the onlookers gasped. "This piece is titled, The Sisters of Solitude, Struggle, and Survival."

The painting was a collage of Black historians, Philly, my mother, and civil rights activists. I didn't know how the predominantly white crowd would take the painting but after a moment of silence, Martin Samuel started a slow clap as Khali followed behind him to get the crowd going. Philly walked up to me and gave me a tearful embrace as did Marissa. I was so taken aback by the reaction because I thought that everyone would hate it.

"I'm so proud of you baby girl. I told you that you could do it." Philly said as she wiped away my tears.

"I love you so much."

"I love you too."

Marissa then added in, "Ms. Massey, I would like to thank you for sharing your touching story with us. I was touched as was everyone else. You are a talent on the rise."

"Yes, she is." Martin Samuel said as he approached all of us. Martin added in, "Madam. I would like to extend my deepest sorrows for your past, but it is your future that is shining brightly. This painting is remarkable, and I would like to extend an offer to possibly purchase it from you."

In my greatest Gary Coleman impersonation I said, "Whatchu talkin about white man?"

"I'm talking about writing you a check and possibly hanging this amazing piece of work in one of my galleries."

"Wait galleries? You own your own galleries there sir?" Philly asked him as she drank her third glass of wine.

"Yes. Three in fact. Samuel Arts. I have three in different parts of California."

"I knew you looked familiar." I said back to him.

"Yes, and your friend here was right. I need to have more respect for your culture. Would you believe that I don't own any African American artwork in my galleries?"

"Actually, I can believe that sir."

"Well, I would like to change that. I would like to make yours the first."

"Are you being serious right now Martin?"

Martin took out his checkbook and wrote out a check to which he handed to me proudly. Would you believe that this man wanted to pay me $200,000 for my painting? I almost had a stroke looking at that amount.

"Oh Lord. I haven't seen these many zeroes since I made that scrapbook with all my ex-boyfriends. Are you being serious? You really want to pay me this much for my work?"

"Yes, I do. We got off to a very rough start, but I want to make sure that our ending is a beautiful."

I looked at my crew and they all seemed to be giving me the approval, which made my decision easier.

"Okay, Martin. I will accept your offer. Only because you need an education on our culture and I feel that my painting can start some interesting conversations inside your gallery. So please, by all means take my work, but when I come into that gallery you better have it on full display."

"That I will, I promise madam."

"Good. Oh, and Martin?"

"Yes, madam?"

"Stop calling me Madam. It's Queen. Or Parker. Got it?"

Martin looked back at me embarrassed with my painting in his hands. "Yes Queen Parker. I'm sorry. Take care."

Martin left with my painting as Philly hugged me tightly by my waist. I couldn't believe that my painting sold just like that, to the least likely buyer at that. I couldn't stop looking at the check. It was a feeling that words couldn't quite describe. I was a rich woman, but I felt wealthier in the soul knowing that my culture took swept somebody off of their feet the way it did.

Khali stood in front as Philly brought me a glass of wine. "Congrats Queen. I'm very happy for you. You deserve this moment. I'm humbled to be in your presence."

I grabbed him by his hand and led him outside where I could finally have him to myself. I had been waiting to since the night of the club. I took him to the roof of the building, where a beautiful view of Los Angeles rested before our eyes. It was a beautiful sight.

"Khali, I know that I seemed odd at the club but I'm very glad that we were able to meet up again."

"I feel the exact way. Your image has been a constant shooting star in my mind. Your face has been a mirage of beauty and delight for my brain to bathe in during the latest hours of the night."

"You spitting poetry again?"

"No, I'm being real."

"Well it's working. It's working a lot."

Khali then grabbed my hand and said to me, "Parker look. I know that both of our journeys may be on different parts of the map, but I would love to find the location to your heart so that I can place mine next to it. Can I have you for one night?"

"In what way?"

"Over a glass of wine and a lobster dinner. My treat."

"Are you asking me on a date Khali?"

"I guess I am."

"You guess?"

"I am. I am asking you on a date Parker."

"Well, it's about damn time."

I grabbed Khali and before I knew what I was doing, I kissed him softly across his chocolate lips. It may have been the wine talking, but I wasn't going to stop myself from basking in this magical moment with him. His lips were as sweet as a piece of Key Lime pie, topped with sexy. Have you ever had such an attraction to someone that you just have no control over what you do next? That's how it was with him.

I pushed him off for a second and said back, "You know what? Let's scratch the dinner at a restaurant. I'll cook for us. I can cook us a lobster dinner, maybe some fondue."

"You sure about that? I don't want to get into your personal space so early."

"No, I'm sure. This is going to seem weird, but I have this feeling of comfort already. I mean, if it seems weird you can just tell me. I can take it."

He placed a hand by my face and said, "No it doesn't seem weird. If you want to have dinner at your house, that is more than fine with me. So, tomorrow night?"

"Tomorrow night."

Khali and I then walked back into the gallery hall where our respective rides were waiting for us. I walked back to Philly's car and he walked back to his guy Avant's car. The entire ride, I was in this trance, my lips were dancing about, and my eyes were gazing at the stars. I couldn't ask for a more magical night.

Philly elbowed me gently as she drove, saying, "You know that I'm so proud of you right?"

"Proud of me?"

"Yes. Girl you ROCKED that showcase. And you're $200,000 richer. I'm damn proud to call you my best friend and my sister. I'm still in shock that ol boy bought that painting from you."

"Yeah, I'm still in shock about that myself."

"So, what did you and Khali talk about on the rooftop? I saw that you two snuck away."

"Yeah, I um, invited him over for dinner tomorrow night. My house."

Philly practically lost her shit in excitement, "WHAAT? You're serious girl?"

"Yes, I'm very serious. Philly am I moving too fast? I mean, I just hate public places and I know it's still early in the game. I hope I'm not moving too fast."

"It all depends on what the end result is. I mean is this just dinner or is it dinner with dessert?"

"That's the thing. I don't want him thinking that I'm going to just strip off all of my clothes for him right away. I've never been physical, so I don't want him thinking that's what the end game is here. I want him to experience romance without having to experience the inside of me. You know?"

"Yeah, I know. Well girl, all I can say is that let the chips fall where they may and take everything slowly. You don't want to move fast. You'll be okay. You're the Queen of romance. If he tries anything, dial my number and I'll come over with my hot pot of grits. I'm serious too."

"I know you are girl, with your crazy ass. As crazy as you want to be. I love you."

"Girl you know it. I love you too."

Chapter Twenty-Two

Philly

Me and Avant were having so much fun together. Every night with him was sensual, passionate, and exciting for my body. Once we got home from Parker's showcase, I had a sexual game night set up with him. I wanted to play Roll the Dice with him, which was a freaky little game I came up with. I bought some dice from Spencer's that had parts of the body and actions on each side. You had to roll twice, one for a body part and one for an action.

So, for example, if you roll an *arm* and then you roll a *kiss* you can kind of get the idea of what to do next.

We were in my living room, with the fireplace kicking, completely naked with the dice. Adina Howard's *T-shirt and Panties* was playing. I had set out some edibles like cut up strawberries, frosting, whipped cream, honey, and sugar to spice things up. I also had some a grapefruit and a fruit roll up for after the game if he was good.

"Okay boo, you roll first." I said to him as I laid on the satin blanket that I had set out.

Avant rolled twice and smiled. "I got lick and I got neck." Avant then took the honey and placed a dab of it on each side of my neck. I closed my eyes as his sopping wet tongue curled onto each side of my neck, rolling across my veins, and making my toes curl. He then widened his lips and sucked the rest of the honey from my warm skin.

It took me a second to actually get up off of the ground, but I did and grabbed the dice for my turn. I rolled them twice as he laid down flat on his back. I was selfishly hoping to get his lips or his dick. After I rolled twice, I gave him a devilish look.

"Hmm," I muttered mysteriously.

"Hmm what? What did you get?"

"I rolled lick and dick." Avant sat up and looked at the dice to make sure I wasn't playing him.

"Oh shit!" he said happily.

"So how do you want it?" I asked while pointing to all of the condiments.

"The grapefruit. I want to see if you can back that shit you were talking earlier with me."

"Oh really? Okay, give me a second."

I took the grapefruit into the kitchen and cut a hole into it that could fit around his dick. My cousin once taught me this trick a while back, and I just never put it to use until now. I allowed the grapefruit to warm up for five seconds so that it could feel warm around his dick and then I brought it back into the living room.

"Close your eyes." I demanded to him before slapping his sexy face.

I then placed the grapefruit around his dick and slid it down his shaft before taking a quick lick of the tip. I then sat back up and shrugged as if to say that was it. Which made him sit back up shocked and angry. I just wanted to test his reaction honestly.

"Um, what the hell are you doing?"

"It said lick nigga, and I licked it. Your turn."

"Come on now."

"Boy I'm just playing. Lay back down."

I flipped the dice over to suck and then forced him back down, so I could finish the job on him. I licked the tip again, slurping some of the acidic juices from around his shaft, and his base before placing my entire mouth onto it. I moved the fruit up and down while sucking as his body shook under my control. I used the grapefruit to fuck him while I sucked him down at the same time.

He let out a manly moan, which got added to my energy level, I loved hearing him moan. I sucked his dick like it was the last time and I enjoyed the taste of the fruit. I was getting all of my nutrients on this night, Vitamin D, and his cum which was healthy in its own way.

Once I was done stealing his soul, Avant took over, sucking honey from my toes, and licking sugar from my abs. He combined the sugar and honey together to rub onto my nipples, licking, sucking, and slurping the sweet combo off of me. His mouth game felt so good, so precise, and so professional.

The next morning, we woke up on the blanket in front of the fireplace; both of us were sticky, full of sin and full of wine. It was the best way to wake up though. I sat up in the mess as his eyes opened up slowly as well.

"Good morning mister."

"Mmm, good morning to you."

"I'm getting tired of you beating this ass up and putting me to sleep sir."

He gave me a sinister laugh and kissed me on the cheek as he stood up. "Well I figured that you take it so well, you were getting used to it."

"Maybe you're right. I'll say maybe so that you don't get too cocky. What do you want for breakfast?"

Avant switched up on me and said, "Instead of you making me breakfast, how about I make you breakfast. What do you want?"

"Well damn, I get breakfast and dick. That's a first."

"Well you're my baby, so I'll do anything for you."

When he said that my eyes popped out of my head and I turned back to look at him.

"You said what?"

He turned around confused. "What do you mean?"

"You called me something. What did you call me?"

"I called you my baby? Is that an issue?"

"Um, actually it kind of is an issue Avant. You calling me that kind of scares me."

"And why is that?"

I stood up and handed him his clothes. "It scares me because it sounds like you're starting to get attached to me. What exactly do you think that this is?"

"What, what is? I'm confused here Philly."

"Us, what do you think we have going on here? Do you think we're in a relationship or something?"

"No, but I thought that's what we were working towards."

"Well you thought wrong sir. That is the opposite of what is going on here. I only wanted sex, not a relationship."

"Okay, you're officially crazy. Like seriously."

I slapped him on the chest angrily before yelling back. "ME? You're the one sitting around here throwing out labels and shit. No, I'm not your baby, I'm not your girlfriend, and I had no plans to be. You're the crazy one."

"Are you that scared of commitment that you're seriously trying to drive me away from you Philly?"

"Drive you away? Nigga please, the car was never in the lot. I think it's time for you to go."

I started to push him towards the door, but he stopped himself to say, "Look, I know that I scared you by calling you baby. But you have to admit that things between us have been fun, hell they've been more than fun. You are an amazing woman Philly. I don't want this to end. Okay? So, let's slow down for a second."

"No, I want you to leave my house. This is over. The sex, the fun, all of it. See you."

"Philly come on now. Don't be like that with me. Not after the night we had last night."

"Well, I hoped you have it saved in your memory, because all of that shit is over with."

I pushed him out of the house and slammed the door behind me. I didn't even know what had come over me, I just snapped. I got so scared by him calling me baby, I didn't realize why, it just brought out the worst in me. I didn't expect for him to get attached to me. I thought we were having sex and that was that.

The worst part is that for the first time ever, I actually cried over a guy. I cried as soon as I slammed the door on him because I knew that the shit was wrong and that he did mean a lot to me. What had I done? I felt so fucked up.

Chapter Twenty-Three

Khali

Later that night

I was nervous as hell pulling up to Parker's house that night. This was my first date in I don't know how long, and for it to be at her house, I was shitting bricks. I didn't want to leave a bad impression on her. I got out of the car with a bouquet of roses and a bottle of pineapple Cîroc just to say I brought something to the date. I know it seemed unconventional, but I tried.

I walked up to the front of the home to see that she was waiting for me at the front door in a sexy, alluring, red dress that made her melanin truly pop.

"Hot damn Ms. Lady, when you show up, you show out."

"You don't look too bad yourself my boy. Are those for me?"

I handed her the gifts, and nodded. "Of course they are. I went to the best flower shop in the city for these."

"Well look at you trying to sweep me off my feet. Come in."

As I walked in, Parker stopped me at the door and showed me her pistol which scared the daylights out of me. She aimed the gun at my head and said, "Just an FYI, I've seen *For Colored Girls* five times and if you try to rape me, I'm putting a bullet in your head and your balls with my uncle's gun. Got it?"

With my hands in the air, I urged, "I'd never do anything like that with you. Number one because I'm no rapist and number two I'm celibate. Sex wasn't even on my mind tonight. I promise. I'd rather make love to your mind. If that's okay with you?"

Parker put the gun down and placed it in her cabinet. Shorty wasn't a game at all. I guess I could see where she was coming from. Her past was a huge detriment to her mind state. Somehow, I always seem to choose the crazy one, this one seemed to be crazy for good reason though.

"Okay." She said with a sigh of relief. "I'm sorry about that. You know with my history and all you can never be too sure about some of you fellas out there."

"It's cool, I think."

Parker grabbed me by the hand and led me to the kitchen where her dinner was set up for us. This woman had gone all out for us. She made lobster tails and steak kabobs. She had a fondue pot of cheese and another fondue pot of chocolate for the fruit and marshmallow platter. I guess this makes up for the whole gun incident.

"Damn woman, it looks like a gourmet restaurant in here. You didn't have to do all of this for me."

"Yes, I did. I told you that I would hook us up and I did. I want you to know that I'm serious about getting to know you. Plus, I hope this makes up for the whole gun situation."

"No, you're good, trust me."

"You sure?"

"I'm positive."

I kissed her lips and I washed my hands so that we could eat. When I say that all of her food tasted like a glimpse of Heaven, I'm not lying. Parker could've been a chef if she wanted to. She even took the Cîroc and made homemade *Pina coladas* with them. Even though her corny ass called them *Parker Coladas.*

"So, I guess this is my way of saying I'm sorry to you." She said as she ate a piece of her fruit.

"Sorry for what? The gun incident?"

"No, well, yes but also for the bus situation a while back. If I would've known you was such a charmer I would've snatched you up back then."

"Well, I guess everything happens for a reason. I mean I'm glad that you gave me the cold shoulder. It set up the future perfectly. I felt like that day was a nightmare intended to set up the beautiful dream later on."

She gazed into my eyes and laughed a bit to herself.

"What?" I asked as I ate a bite of steak.

"You. You're unlike anyone that I've ever dated, met, or interacted with ever. My best friend Philly always told me that guys like you only existed in Cosmo or the movies. I guess not. You better not be playing me Khali."

"Trust me Parker, playing you is the least of my intentions. I'm getting tired of getting tired of being played myself. I've been getting like a video game controller for half of my life."

"Well, I don't play games. I don't play games at all."

"That's good to know, because I figured you were an all business type of woman."

"Yes I am. So, tell me Khali, why did you choose to be celibate? Like what influenced that decision?"

I took a deep breath as I looked at the tattoo with my first child's name. I looked back at her with solemn eyes and said bravely, "Heartbreak."

"Heartbreak?"

"Yes heartbreak. I once dated this girl named Jhene. Back in my sex fiend days and we got busy like it was our duty. So, when the obvious result happened, which was her pregnancy, I was elated. I was going to bring a man into this world that would be the future."

"What happened?"

"Jhene didn't see it that way because she aborted the baby and essentially broke my heart. I had gotten this tattoo done and everything. I chose to keep it to remind myself of the pain that she caused. I will never forget it. So, I made the conscientious decision to abort sex until I met a woman that I felt that I could start a real family with one day."

Parker got up from her chair with tears in her eyes and hugged me around my neck. I could see that my story had truly touched her soul. I began to cry myself as we embraced in my seat.

"Hey." She said as she wiped away my tears. "I promise you, that I would never hurt you like that. Ever. She had to be the worst type of person to do that to you. You are a great man and trust me you will make a great family man one day. I truly believe that in my heart of hearts."

We continued to hug as inside of my mind, I already felt as though I had met the woman that I would want to start a family with. She was the epitome of everything that I wanted, needed, and craved in a woman which made my connection to her feel so much better.

"Hey Parker,"

"Yes."

"I want to ask you something, if you say no, I won't blame you."

"It depends on what you're about to ask me sir."

"How would you like to go to Coney Island with me and my sister Kindness in four months? We went a day ago, but I promised that I would take her back before her graduation. I would love for you to meet her."

"Coney Island? Four months," she asked while giving it extreme thought.

"If you don't want to go, I'll understand."

"I would love to. If you can answer one question for me," she said without another moment of thought.

"And that question would be."

She placed a hand across my thick beard and asked, "How do you know we'll last four months?"

"Because when God walks you through a door, you don't close it. You walk right through it, you close it behind you, and you embrace what was behind it initially."

Parker's adorable blush basked under the light as she said, "You always know what to say Khali Carter."

"So is that a yes to Coney Island."

"That's a hell yes to Coney Island."

"Well damn. That went better than I thought it would. But can you leave the gun at home though?"

Parker laughed and nodded with her adorable teeth glowing back at me. "Yes. I'll leave the gun at home Khali."

The rest of the night, we sat, ate dinner, and painted portraits over 90's R&B music. This was the love making that I craved, the sensual, mind numbing, non-physical lovemaking that I desired because it meant more than sex. I was literally bonding with this woman, and I couldn't have been happier.

I felt like I had finally found the woman that I could start a real future with, it was an amazing feeling. Parker Massey was a gift from God, and I was going to cherish her as such. She was the Black Queen that every man should die to have on their arm, and she was truly one of a kind. I just hoped she wouldn't pull any more guns on a brotha. That was pretty damn scary I'll have to admit.

Chapter Twenty-Four

Avant

Two Days Later

Philly and I were still not on talking terms since our big blow up at her house. It had been two whole days. She had flipped out so badly, I didn't know how to approach her any level. It was especially odd at work because every time we would enter the elevator together, she would act as if she didn't know me. It sucked because I had plans to make her my date at the Essence Festival that was coming up but since that happened I guess the shit was dead as a doorknob.

I sat in my office in a funk, my mood was so bad that I was mugging everybody that came around to me.

Philly was on my mind every hour of the day, and I was going crazy thinking about her. I had to find a way to get my mind off of her, maybe if I went down to floor three to talk to her so we could get things back on the right path. I left my desk, but I was grabbed by Javari forcefully.

I pulled away from him and yelled, "Get your hands off of me. Are you crazy?"

Hating ass Javari said back, "Where the hell do you think you're going?"

"To take a break if you don't mind nigga, move away from me."

"You don't get a break right now. Go back to your seat."

"Nigga you are not my boss! Get the fuck back before I chin check your ass."

We were about to go to blows until Cheryl stepped in between us. "Hey. What is going on with you two?"

"This fucker thinks he can tell me what to do. He's not my boss, you are."

"Cheryl, I'm just trying to officiate some sense and control. This cat thinks because he's new that he can just do whatever he wants to. We have work to do."

Cheryl looked at us both before saying in response, "Okay. You're both right. But Javari, I'm going to need you to stop messing with Avant. He's new here and it seems that you've had it out for him since he started with us. This is the second time I've had to step in between you two and there will NOT be a third time. You understand? Javari, I'm really talking to you. You're a vet here, I expect more out of you."

Cheryl then pulled me away from the chaos and back into my office. "I apologize on behalf of Javari. I'm about one day from dropping him. He's getting on my nerves. But, Avant what's going on with you? You've been very irritable the last few days. If you don't mind me asking, is everything okay at home? I mean you don't have to say anything to me if you don't want to, but it just seems that something is truly bothering you."

I sat back in my chair and buried my face in my hands. "Cheryl, I just, I just have this issue with a significant other that's getting on my last nerve."

"Ahh," she said as she said down next to me. "I know all about significant others. Come on, tell your buddy what's up."

"Have you ever wanted somebody to feel the way that you feel, even when you know that they won't?"

"Yes, I've had a few instances like that. But look Avant, us women, we're complex characters. Just when you think you have all of the answers we change the questions. We will keep you guessing. So, it seems that this lady friend has been changing up the questions on you. Which is likely her way of trying to protect her feelings. It'll work itself out. Trust me."

"I sure hope so. I really like this woman Cheryl. I truly do."

"I can see it in your eyes that you do. I can feel it when you talk. But you can't let it drive you insane. Keep faith and remain patient. Trust me, things will work themselves out. If they don't, someone else will be there to pick up the pieces. I'll tell you what. How about you take the rest of the day off and think about things. Cool off and then I'll see you at the Essence Festival."

I got up and hugged Cheryl as I said, "Thanks boss. I really appreciate it. More than you know."

She said, "Hey don't mention it. There aren't many men like you left, I want you to remain sane for the Queen who has your heart. I'll be praying for you Avant."

Chapter Twenty-Five

Philly

Philly's Office

"So, you just kicked him out of your house?"

My cousin Janae was so pissed off at me for allowing Avant out of my life, she looked like she wanted to punch me straight in the mouth.

"Yep. I did what was best for me. He was getting way too attached to me."

"Girl he was digging you on a level above sex. Why do you always do that Philly? Why do you always allow yourself to end up in these situations where you end up alone?"

"Because I like being alone?"

"Why? That was a good man, a sexy man, a man worth having. You kicked him out like yesterday's trash because he called out an affectionate nickname? You're crazy. Like straight up."

"I did what was best for me. You wouldn't understand that."

"Yes, I can. If anybody can understand that, it's me. I've been rocking with you for how long now? I know when you really like somebody Philly. You really like that man. He stole your soul and then he stole your heart. You just don't want to admit it. You're so used to never being in love or really caring for anybody that you got scared by his presence. You got scared because what was supposed to be a one-night stand ended up being more than that. Admit girl. You are in love with that boy."

I stood up out of my chair and started to pack up my things in anger. I grabbed my purse and started to walk out before she grabbed me, "Girl what did I say? Why are you leaving?"

"I'm leaving because you're pissing me off."

"How am I pissing you off?"

"You're pissing me off because you're right."

I took off out of the office and up to the fifth floor where Avant's office was. Janae was right on the money. I was digging Avant more than I thought that I was. I had let that man come in my life and steal my heart with his charming ass. I had never felt the way that I did about him. I had to find him and let him know that I did want him.

I saw Cheryl standing by her water bubbler and I poked her on the shoulder, "Hey, have you seen Avant?"

Cheryl said back in return, "Um, no, I haven't actually I just sent him home. He was having a bad day."

"Dammit. Okay."

As I started to leave, Cheryl called out to me. "Hey Philly,"

"Yes?" I asked turning back around.

"Go get him. He really likes you."

I smiled and walked to the elevator in a rush. As I got in, I heard a voice beckon out, "Hold that elevator for me."

I did and once I saw who entered it, I got upset that I did. Javari, supreme taco breath himself, entered the elevator. He was such a creep. His creep meter was elevating consistently.

"What's up Philly? I see you were on my floor. Looking for me?"

"No, but I see your breath still smells like a cesspool, still looking for that breath mint?"

"Come on girl, when are we going to stop playing these games."

"Games? Baby boy you're the type of game that I'd leave on pause."

I stormed off of the elevator and through the doors of the entrance as he followed closely behind me. I was hoping that Avant hadn't left yet, I couldn't miss him. As I reached the parking lot, Javari's creepy ass was behind me still trying to get my attention.

"Why are you following me dude?" I asked to him impatiently.

"Because I know you want me the same way that I want you." At this point, he was so close to me that I had to back up into my car. I was starting to fear that this dude was on a mission that wouldn't be stopped.

"Boy, back up off of me."

"Or what?"

"Or I'll call security."

"And? I'll pay them off."

Javari started grabbing me roughly by my arm, trying to reach under my skirt. I slapped him, but he slapped me back. He slapped me so hard that he knocked me backwards into my car. At that point, I started to scream help. This dude was really trying to rape me in front of the job.

"Somebody HELP!" I saw him unzip his pants and when he did, I felt a figure rush over to grab him.

It was Avant. My hero. Avant rushed over like a Black Hercules right as things were about to get bad. Javari looked like he seen a ghost when Avant grabbed him.

I watched as Avant beat Javari all over the parking lot. He beat him to the point that he left him a bloody mess. Avant body slammed Javari onto his car and choked him until Javari ran out of sight.

"Stay away from her, fuckin coward."

Once Avant knew that he was gone, he came over to me to make sure that I was okay.

"You good?"

"Yeah." I said as I hugged him with my tears in my eyes. "You saved my life."

"Of course." Avant's smile then turned to a frown as he backed away from me. He was still very much upset with me. He just didn't want to see Javari attacking me. I don't know where he came from, but I was glad he came.

"Avant, wait." I called out to him to make him turn around. "I'm sorry."

"I don't want to hear it Philly. Just get in your car and leave. I'm going to get drinks to get my mind off you. This is what you've done to me. You have me trying to erase your memory by getting drunk off of my ass at Club Joi. So, thanks a lot." Avant then got into his car angrily and left me there standing in tears.

What was I saying? I was totally feeling this man. I was head over hills for this man. After what I seen for him, I just wanted to be in his arms, I wanted him to pick me up and take me into his arms like the Superman that he was. When I watched Avant dip out into his car, I knew that I had to fight for him. I had to fight for him the same way that most would fight for a promotion. I had to fight for him the same way that most would fight for the last piece of Grandma's fried chicken during dinner.

As much as it pains me to say it, Janae was right about everything she said. It was time for me to grow up and realize that I wasn't getting any younger. I was so scared to let anyone into my bubble because of a fear that some of my inner darkest secrets would scare them away.

In all honesty, Avant was worth it. Avant was worth the pain, he was worth the time, and he was worth the stress. I was going to give my all to Avant, something I'd never done with any man ever. I just hoped that he would accept my flaws.

So, with that said, if Avant was going to be at *Club Joi,* I would be there too.

Chapter Twenty-Five

Avant

Club Joi

I guess this was my life, getting drunk inside of a club to erase my mind of Philly. I had to work with her but that didn't mean that I had to show her anymore love. It's fitting that in the same place where we met. I was now here again alone to try to rid myself of her stink forever. I had two beers and I was planning to have five more before I even thought about leaving the Club.

As I drank my life away, I felt a brush against my shoulder and a voice leaned in close to me.

"Avant? I thought that was you."

I looked up to see a mesmerizing body of grace staring back at me. It was Teri, the same Teri from the plane when I first arrived in Los Angeles.

"Teri?"

"Yes, it's me." She said with a smile and a tight hug. Teri looked damn good, in her tight blue dress, her brown hair was down to her shoulders, and she resembled a younger Toni Braxton. She looked good on the plane but looked even tastier now.

"Well isn't this a surprise." She said with her eyes dead set onto me.

"Yeah, I would've never expected to see you here."

"Well, I'm actually here with a client but now that I see you, I have a better reason for staying."

"Oh, is that so?" I asked scooting closer.

"Yes, it is. You remember what I said to you the last time we saw each other."

"That if we saw each other again, it would be fate?"

"Yep. And here we are. Together again. So, tell me Avant. What are you doing here all by yourself?"

"Just doing some drinking. The better question is am I leaving alone?"

Teri smiled and looked back at me, "That's up to you."

I thought about it closely. I mean, I thought about her statement VERY CLOSELY. Now on one hand, Philly had pissed me off something major and even though I stopped that creepy ass Javari from taken advantage of her, I was still unsure about her.

On the second hand, Teri looked like she was full of enough vodka, pomp and circumstance to make love to me right there by the bar. Teri was quite the looker, no doubt about it but I wasn't the urge to bang her life away out of frustration. It was tempting but I was still running myself ragged thinking about Philly, no amount of alcohol could change that. So ultimately, I had no plans to fuck Teri, as great as she looked. I was going to have to decline her offer.

Before I could even answer, the DJ suddenly stopped the music and said over the loud speaker, "Um excuse me, is there a writer by the name of Avant Moore here?"

The entire club seemed to turn to me at the bar and I reluctantly raised my hand. The DJ then saluted me and said, "Well this song is dedicated to you then."

All of a sudden, Sean Paul's *Give It Up to Me* began to play and the crowd on the dance floor began to separate until one woman stood by herself. It was Philly. Philly was wearing a similar dress to the one she wore the night we met. She told me to come to her with her finger and after looking back at Teri, I slowly came to her on the dance floor. Could you blame me?

Teri shrugged and began to talk to another guy as Philly pulled me to her by my collar.

"Did you really think I would let you get away from me?"

She then pushed me away and danced provocatively towards me in the same way that she did during our first dance. She grinded her hips on my waist, and then said in my ear, "You are everything that I've ever wanted, and I refuse to let another bitch have you."

I twirled her around and then replied with, "You sure about that?"

Philly placed one of her legs on my hip as I dipped her, then she said, "You're damn right."

As the song played, we danced our night away and Philly made an effort to dance in a way that told every woman in the club including Teri, that I belonged to her. I held tightly enough that the men, she was mine. Once our eyes made contact, she mouthed the words *I love you* to me and I grabbed her by the throat to kiss her passionately. I then said *I love you too* and we hugged as the song came to an end. I guess it was the perfect way for things to happen. In the same club that brought us together, we made things official. It's crazy how things go in life, I was literally in L.A. for what seemed like a month now, but damn what a month it's been.

After the song ended, I was so ready to explore Philly's mind to see where her head was. We had gone through the craziest month that I will never forget. Philly and I grabbed each other's hands as I walked her from the dance floor. We sat down outside on the patio area, where she sat on my lap, and kissed me all over my face. This was the affectionate side of Philly that I wasn't used to outside of the bedroom. I could see a change over Philly as she sat across me. Gone was the feeling that she didn't want me around, gone was the need for sex but so complete solitude, Philly was all mine.

I grabbed her hand and exclaimed to her, "I'm not going to lie to you, I never saw this coming."

"I told you that I'm full of surprises Avant." She said back with her face glowing in confidence and relief at the same time. Her facial expressions, her closeness to me, it all brought this warmth to my body that I hadn't had since my ex.

She then continued, "Did you really think you could get rid of me. Especially after what you did for me today?"

"I thought you didn't give a shit about me honestly."

"I never said that I didn't give a shit about you Avant."

"That's how you made it feel when slammed the door in my face like a Jehovah's Witness."

"Well that wasn't the case. I was scared Avant. You started throwing around affectionate nicknames and I knew you were getting attached to me. I couldn't have you getting attached because that would mean you would want a relationship."

"And what was a relationship so scary for you Philly? Am I not enough of a man for you?"

"Don't put words in my mouth."

"That's just how it seemed to me."

Philly grabbed my mouth aggressively. "Listen here sir. I want you to listen to me very clearly. I've never felt the way that I feel about you for any guy ever. Not the Skills guy, not the guy who used to like sucking mustard off of my toes for some odd reason and not even the old guy who wanted me to be his sugar mama in his mansion. You, Avant, have changed my life in more ways than one. I know that seems hard to believe but every moment with you has me feeling like nothing can go wrong."

"So, what are we waiting for? Huh? What are you scared of Philly?"

"I CAN'T HAVE KIDS!" She said abundantly. No matter how much noise was around us when she said that everything seemed to go silent around us. Philly looked at me like she was waiting for me to get up and leave her right there.

Philly then continued, "I was told two years ago that I have a PCOS which is polycystic ovarian syndrome. It affects my infertility so as much as I love sex, there is no end result if you wanted more. So, what's up? Now you know my biggest and darkest secret. Something that nobody in the world knows not even my best friend. That's why I never get in relationships. Most men see a future that has kids in it, which I can't give them. So, the question that now rest is, am I really worth the trouble?"

I grabbed her hand as tightly as I could while looking her in her beautiful eyes. Her touch was so powerful. I wiped away the tears that was drowning both of her eyes as I said, "Philly, when I met you, I wasn't like I thought our one-night stand was just that. But after spending time with you and getting to know you, I know that there is nothing perfect about you at all. But guess what, there's nothing perfect about me either. But that's the beauty of a relationship. Nothing is ever perfect. Not every day will be full of sun, sometimes we'll have to stand in the storm together. But rest assured Philly, I will stand in a ring of fire just to be with you. If you promise to never give up on me and be my Queen. I love you Philly."

"I love you too mister." Philly kissed me passionately as we then embraced. I was honored to be her first true love and her man. I guess it all truly worked out.

Chapter Twenty-Six

Parker

Two Months Later

I had never been to Coney Island before but going with Khali and his sister Kindness was more fun than I ever expected. Kindness was something else, she was a gift, and her future was something to behold. I was having fun with them even though Khali just left me and Kindness sitting by the Ferris wheel. He claimed that he forgot something in the car.

"Can you believe that Khali just left us sitting here?" I said to Kindness as she at her cotton candy.

"Yeah, he's something else. I'll tell you whatever he's getting from the car better be damn important."

"Right?! Well since we're here, I just want to say congrats on your graduation ahead of time. You're going to change the world I can see it now."

"Thanks Parker." She said as her chocolate skin glowed in the sun. "I hope to not only change the world, but also change the way people see us. I want to exemplify black excellence and black girl magic for years to come."

Kindness then looked over and pointed to someone, "Hey. Don't you know them?"

I looked up to see Philly and Avant walking towards us holding hands.

"What the hell are you two doing here?"

Philly then said, "What? I can't take my boyfriend to see sights? I mean he is like the first real boyfriend I've ever had."

"I see that but you two being here seems…"

I then saw her cousin Janae walking towards us too, and then my fucking mother who was also with Khali's mother. Now I was starting to worry, this seemed pretty damn coincidental.

"Um, what is going on here?" I asked as everyone began to surround me.

I then heard Khali's voice behind say, "I invited them." I turned to see him with his hands behind his back.

"Khali, what are you doing?"

Khali put a finger to his lips and shook his head, "I wrote you a poem. You want to hear it?"

As tears began to fill my eyes, I nodded, Philly began to record from her phone as Kindness and her soft voice began to hum a melody. Khali stepped up and began to recite his poem to me.

Black Love is everything to me

It's the R&B song that I keep on repeat

It's the first and last piece of chocolate inside a heart shaped box

It's the flow of water coming from the sea

Black Love is the greatest sight that you'll ever see.

Parker, you are the epitome of an everlasting lottery ticket

No matter times you win, you feel like it's the first time.

Basically, I fall in love with you every day like it's my first time.

You are the greatest sweetest tempo, and the greatest rhyme

You are the center of time

You are the daylight. You are the night, you are the stars.

You are the Earth, Jupiter, Venus, and Mars

You are nature's finest creation

You are a gift to me

You are summer time fine.

So, without wasting any more time Khali then got down on one knee as the tears began to flow from my eyes.

"Parker Massey will you marry me and promise to always be mine?"

I kneeled down next to him and kissed him almost to death as I nodded yes. Khali slipped the ring that was as big as the Grand Canyon on my finger. I didn't want to let go of my grip around his neck as everyone around us began to clap and cry as Philly hugged me.

After years of dreaming of a life that was different than the one that I was used to, I finally found my prince charming. It's amazing what can happen when your prayers are presented back to you full force. It almost seemed unreal when Khali popped the question, but it was a moment that will stick with me for the rest of my life.

The fact that Khali accepted everything about me from my size, to my virginity to my good girl nature told me that he was the one for me. He was my knight in shining armor, and he was my everlasting memory. I love this man, and with his ring, I would love him forever.

If I learned anything from my experience, and from watching Philly finally make things official with someone, it was that Black Love is real. Black Love is a presence unlike any other. Black Love is magical. And most importantly, Black Love Matters.

Holy matrimony

One Year later

Chapter Twenty-Seven

Parker

October 17, 2019

    I would've never expected this. I was only minutes away from marrying the king that God had been saving for me. It seemed to be a dream that I was afraid to wake up from. An illusion of sorts. I stood in the mirror of my hotel's bathroom turned make shift dressing room for hours staring at myself. Khali wanted to have a different type of wedding, a private wedding, one with only our parents and our friends inside of a small church. I was still nervous as hell, my legs were shaking, my stomach was doing this uncontrollable dance that I couldn't seem to shake, I was all over the place.

    My satin white dress was giving me life though, a life that I needed desperately because every moment of awaiting my destiny was giving me a shortness of breath. If it wasn't for my babes, Philly coming in with her elegant glow to comfort me, I would've lost my mind.

"Hey girl? It's almost showtime. You ready to do this?"

She could see in my face that I was losing my marbles, well the marbles that I still had inside of my whacked-out mind.

"Girl, why does this man want to marry me?" I asked as I flailed my arms with a sense of fear mixed with doubt in my voice.

"Why?" she asked while looking at me with a disappointment glare. "Girl, look at you. You're beautiful. Beautiful doesn't deserve to be in the same category as you. If he doesn't marry you, I will."

We shared a laugh, a laugh I truly needed at that moment. Philly knew that I wanted to tie the knot more than anything. I was just going through one of many panic attacks.

Philly then added in, "Say, you remember when we were a bit younger, and we envisioned what our perfect guy would like? I always wanted my perfect guy to be this mix of Usher and Bill Bellamy. But you, you always wanted that strong, black king that you believed would change the world. You held out hope for him to come, and you never stopped believing that he would one day show up."

I watched Philly begin to choke up, a faint tear fell from her right eye, "Girl. I shouldn't be crying right now because I spent way too much money on this damn makeup, but I'm so fucking happy for you right now. I've watched you go through so much in your life. I've watched you deal with some of the weakest men that this city offers. I've watched you grow up so much and let me tell you, this is your moment. You deserve this moment. You deserve this man. The same way that Avant has changed me, is the same way that I see Khali changing you. So, like I said before, you better go out there and marry that man."

Our hug that followed next was one of sisterhood, of love, and of trust. Philly may have been a sex crazed sistah with her pretty head in the clouds, but she never let me down.

"I love you girl. Maybe, next year Avant and you will be walking you down the aisle."

"Oop, girl, you swear." She said jokingly before her face became serious. "But in actuality, I would love to marry that man one day. Just like I would love to have his child, sadly, I don't know what man would want to marry a woman who can't produce children."

"Oh girl, stop it!" I said commandingly. "He loves you, and if he's still with you now, obviously he's not worried about that. Trust me that man is for you Philly."

Philly then cut me, "Well this isn't about me anyway. This about you. This is your night."

"You're right, you're right."

"Go out there and get married girl. Dry those tears."

In the background, I could hear the song chosen for our ceremony beginning to play. Teddy Pendergrass' *Latest and Greatest Inspiration.* We looked at each other and she held her hand out for me, I grabbed it tightly. The lyrics to the song spoke to my soul so much as we both walked to the entrance of the church where my fiancée awaited.

> *"I've been so many places*
> *I've seen so many things*
> *But none quite as lovely as you*
> *More beautiful than the Mona Lisa*
> *Worth more than gold*
> *And my eyes have the pleasure to behold*
> *You're my latest and my greatest*
> *My latest, my greatest inspiration*
> *Things never looked clearer*
> *Peace within never felt nearer."*

Philly was right, I had been through so much in life. I had been abused by my own father; I still had the scars from his attacks. I still have emotional scars from the dogs that I had dated in my past. But now, that suffering was all over. This was my time, this was my moment, I was about to marry my prince charming. In front of my family, my friends, and my God, I was about to become Mrs. Khali Carter.

Chapter Twenty-Eight

Khali

I couldn't help but be swept up in emotion. I was watching my everything come down the aisle to become my eternal blessing. Her walk was elegant. Her dress gave her the image the angels that would come to me in my dreams would give. She was the embodiment of Heaven. Her walking down the aisle to *Latest, and Greatest Inspiration* made everything sweeter for me. I remember when my father would dance with my mother to that song every night he'd come from work.

I would often sit in the front room watching them, wondering if that type of love existed for me one day. I loved their love, that black love, that sweet, harmonious ecstasy that brought goose bumps to my arms. Now, my mother was in the front row of my wedding, ready to see me become the King to my Queen that my dad was to her.

You know it's funny how life can bring someone to you when you least expect it. Had I known that the same woman who gave me the cold shoulder on a bus one day would be the same woman I'd be marrying, I would've replayed that moment over and over again. I guess the best thing about this, is that after years of being hurt, and left on the street to die of heartbreak, I've finally found the one for me.

She was the greatest gift that anyone could ask for. She was my foundation, my everyday Christmas gift. Here she was now, in my face, moments from taking away the pain of a thousand souls who hurt us both before. I grabbed onto her hands, and I never stopped looking into her eyes the entire ceremony. Even when my tears burned them as they dripped onto my tuxedo, my eyes remained locked on her. Even when the pastor asked for my vows and I said in full honesty.

Parker Massey, when I met you, I was nothing more than a poetic hopeless romantic. I had my heartbroken in the worst of ways, and honestly, I'd rewind the clock to allow it to be broken again. If only so that I could replay the moment after, when I first laid eyes on you. There you were; all beautiful, reading Sistah Souljah, and not giving me any type of play. But what I didn't know, was that inside, your heart was enclosed. Now here we stand today, I'm yours and your mine. When I say that you are the best thing to happen to me, I mean that, I really do. So, with this ring, I promise to you that I will forever be your King, your hero, your medicine, and your husband. I promise to hold your heart in my hand, and keep it in a safe place, which is right next to mine.

My eyes never left hers, my eyes never left hers. Our kiss seemed to last forever when the Pastor gave me the honor of kissing my bride, hell I would've stopped the clock myself just to kiss her eternally. Parker Massey Carter. That massaged my tongue whenever I said it. Parker Massey Carter. My bride. My pride. My life. As we took our walk up the aisle to our limo, I remember looking up to the sky to the Lord above, wondering why he ended the world so quickly because this for damn sure seemed like Heaven.

Maybe it was. Now all there was left to do was solidify it with our honeymoon. And it was a honeymoon that I would live in my heart until it stopped beating.

Have you ever had sex so good that it seemed almost like a dream or an afflicted fantasy that was good for the mind, body, and soul?

That's how good it felt as I made love to my newly christened wife Parker in between the sands of Maui, Hawaii on our honeymoon. I would go to the ends of the Earth just to be with her. Hell, if could carry the Earth on my shoulders to give to her, I would.

The memory of her smile as we kissed in front of the world will forever be entrenched. However, the smile that she had that night as we walked across the beach with our toes buried deep into the salmon orange sand was too beautiful for words. Parker's smile could bring life to the million and one still hearts that her beauty snatched life away from.

My Queen also had this insatiable glow to her cocoa brown skin that could outshine the moonlight and it was a magnificent sight to behold as we walked to a spot that I had picked out just for us. I wanted this night to be one that she would never forget for the rest of her life. I wanted to be the memory that she rehashed to when civilians would ask her why her smile was glued to her face.

"Baby, where are you taking me?"

"Just to this little spot, we're almost there."

She stopped to glare deeply into the seductive view of the Pacific, as her fingers locked between mine.

"This so gorgeous. I can't believe we're finally here. This feels like home."

I turned her around looking deep into her eyes that were always a mysteriously captivating deep shade of green.

"No matter where, no matter the distance, anywhere I go will always feel like home to me as long as I'm with you."

I placed a few kisses across your shoulders breathing in the insatiable smell of her fragrance, so like that of vanilla. I then left a peck on your forehead before continuing our walk across Makena beach, the only beach that didn't care if you were clothed. Once we arrived at the spot, my chocolate drop blushed at the sight of rose petals and aroma therapy candles surrounding a silk blanket with our wedding picture in the middle.

Inside of a picnic basket were strawberries as ripe and as sweet as her kisses, a can of whipped cream and heart racing chocolate dipping sauce. Of course, I also had her favorite bottle of Pinot Noir and two wine glasses. Parker was as speechless as the first time that I had met her; she was falling in love all over again.

"You didn't do this all for me, this is amazing."

I pulled her close to me, close enough that our hearts were practically playing tag with one another and our body's warmth soothed our pores.

"Like I told you at the wedding, your happiness is what I seek refuge in. It's my personal ecstasy."

We kissed, her lips were sweet enough to cause a sugar rush and take my body on a roller coaster ride of sensual magic.

"Come here baby, sit with me." She sat near me as we enjoyed each-others company, expressing our greatest fears and greatest hopes for our lives as the sunset made love to our eyes. She then looked at me with her soul snatching glare, kissing me a couple of times across my chin and cheek.

Parker took one of the strawberries and fed it to me, the juice from the plump fruit flew across the blanket, and then she bit into it before kissing me. My wife's lips outmatched the sweet nectar from the strawberry, but together they created a mystical explosion that drove me insane.

The way Parker then sat across my waist, grinding with her curvy shape, and fed me another strawberry out of her mouth made my blood ascend to a temperature hotter than a Hawaiian volcano. I loved her scrumptious curves, she was all woman.

"You're my everything." She whispered to me softly under the warm Maui skies as she kissed my pecs with a passionate precision. Parker's tongue danced so fluently across my chest that it was like she was trying to leave a tattoo on it with her saliva.

The way that she kissed her way from my chest to my neck, hitting that spot in the corner rejuvenated a soul once trapped in a cell of lost hope. She sent shockwaves to my body by tongue kissing me, the taste from our fruit filled late snack made me want to devour her lips, my hands were pressed hard against her ass.

The light pink bikini she was wearing already made it easy to exploit her body, touching across her silky skin. The red sky watched us like a movie as our skin, our souls bled into each other, leaving our memories dancing amongst the tidal waves of the sea as she toppled me, laying me on my back.

The more that her lips grazed my skin, the harder that my dick became inside of my shorts that she eventually pulled from me with her teeth.

As midnight dawned upon us, we bathed in the darkness and drowned in our appetite for one another. Once inside of her as she rode me, I let out a groan that could match the howls from the wolves. The methodical way that she rotated around with her hips as my dick went deeper into her was such a satisfying feeling.

Once I flipped her over allowing her back to maneuver the sand that was cotton soft, I told her that she was my soulmate in her ear before grinding deeply into her. She called out to me and to the sky above, her nails dug deep into me, her legs were wrapped tightly around me.

She didn't want this to end and neither did I.

As we created a memory that would last forever on that island, we also procreated a part of our lives that would last even after our last breath. That night, under the calming moon and sexy midnight blanket of color, we created a gift that neither of us deserved. It was her first time, and my first time making love to someone who really had my heart. This was the love that I sought; this was the Black Love that I craved.

It was truly a night inside of Heaven on the beaches of Maui and nine months later, we were able to see it all come to fruition again.

I love you Paishance. Welcome to the world my princess…

The End

Stay Blessed.

Author Quardeay